# ONCE UPON A DUKE'S DREAM

## HAPPILY EVER AFTER BOOK 3

### ELLIE ST. CLAIR

♥ **Copyright 2017 by Ellie St Clair**

**All rights reserved.**

This book or parts thereof may not be reproduced in any form, stored in any retrieval system, or transmitted in any form by any means—electronic, mechanical, photocopy, recording, or otherwise—without prior written permission of the publisher.

Facebook: Ellie St. Clair

Cover by AJF Designs

Do you love historical romance? Receive access to a free ebook, as well as exclusive content such as giveaways, contests, freebies and advance notice of pre-orders through my mailing list!

Sign up here!

**Also By Ellie St. Clair**

*Happily Ever After*
The Duke She Wished For
Someday Her Duke Will Come
Once Upon a Duke's Dream
He's a Duke, But I Love Him
Loved by the Viscount
Because the Earl Loved Me

Happily Ever After Box Set Books 1-3
Happily Ever After Box Set Books 4-6

For a full list of all of Ellie's books, please see
www.elliestclair.com/books.

# CONTENTS

| | |
|---|---|
| Prologue | 1 |
| Chapter 1 | 5 |
| Chapter 2 | 10 |
| Chapter 3 | 19 |
| Chapter 4 | 28 |
| Chapter 5 | 36 |
| Chapter 6 | 42 |
| Chapter 7 | 51 |
| Chapter 8 | 61 |
| Chapter 9 | 69 |
| Chapter 10 | 76 |
| Chapter 11 | 84 |
| Chapter 12 | 92 |
| Chapter 13 | 105 |
| Chapter 14 | 113 |
| Chapter 15 | 120 |
| Chapter 16 | 126 |
| Chapter 17 | 131 |
| Chapter 18 | 138 |
| Chapter 19 | 145 |
| Chapter 20 | 153 |
| Epilogue | 162 |
| An excerpt from He's a Duke, But I Love Him | 167 |
| *Also by Ellie St. Clair* | 177 |
| *About the Author* | 181 |

# PROLOGUE

*B*radley flicked the reins of his horse, pushing him to run even faster as the large manor came into sight. He glanced over at the second horse keeping time beside him, most concerned about the look of the man who was thrown over the saddle. Roger didn't move, but the light rise and fall of his chest gave Bradley hope.

His heart pounding nearly in time with the rhythm of the horse's hooves, Bradley Hainsworth, Duke of Carrington, raced the horses up the drive, but went around the back of the palatial manor house to the servants' entrance, as was fitting the situation. He vaulted off his horse, ran to the house and pounded loudly until finally a servant opened the door, an incredulous look on his face as he took in Bradley's blood-stained cloak, windswept hair, and the crazed look in his eye.

"Are you here for the house party? I believe, sir, you may have the wrong entrance…"

While the butler clearly didn't know who he was, he had seemed to discern from his dress that he did not belong at the servant's entrance. Bradley, however, had no time for explanations.

"My friend is gravely injured. Send for the physician at once, and find a man to help me bring him inside to a place where he can be treated," Bradley commanded.

As the servant began walking away, Bradley called out after him, "Oh! And find Alexander Landon, Duke of Barre!"

The man recognized his words with a slight nod of his head. He had likely already been on his way to find the master of the house.

With the help of a footman, Bradley carried Roger inside, placing him on a small couch in a room in the servants' quarters that was clean and comfortable enough. He helped the servants who began bustling about, tearing away Roger's shirt, and he grimaced at the hole the bullet had made in his friend's chest.

Their old friend the Duke of Barre finally appeared in the doorway, his face aghast as he took in what was in front of him.

"My God, Carrington! What in the...?"

"I've not much time to explain, but I was helping Roger escape from France, where he had been falsely imprisoned. We were on our way back to England when we were ambushed," Bradley said in a rush. "I must apologize for imposing on you like this, but we were so close to Warfield and I didn't know where else to go."

"It's fine," Alexander replied. "I'm glad you felt you could trust me."

A servant called to Alexander from the doorway, and he turned to Bradley. "I'll return shortly," he said. "The physician should be here momentarily."

Bradley nodded, and now that he had time to consider all that had happened, guilt began to descend onto his shoulders.

For this was all his fault.

He recalled the day he had agreed to help the Foreign Office with their request. They could not infiltrate the highest ranks of society without drawing attention to themselves, but they were concerned that there were gentlemen who were passing on information to the French. Of course, there were more than a few Frenchmen within society, although every one of them made it more than clear that their allegiance was with the English. They had all lived in England for some time and had not returned to France in a number of years, meaning that suspicion about their loyalty was not often questioned. Bradley had agreed to assist the Foreign Office in watching such gentlemen, but, until his trip to Paris, nothing had been of note.

Roger had been eager to help, and volunteered to travel to Paris to see what he could discover.

Bradley realized that someone knew who they were and what they were doing for the Foreign Office, although he did not know how they had discovered such things. Perhaps Roger had let it slip, although that was highly doubtful given how trusted a friend he had been. Regardless, Roger's capture and imprisonment in France had led to Bradley traveling to the continent to help his friend return to England, and things had only grown more complicated from there.

There had been strange circumstances that had placed Roger under guard in the first instance, for his friend had been arrested for stealing, despite the fact he would never have pilfered a single thing. Bradley knew Roger, the son of an earl and his boyhood friend, better than anyone.

Roger had been shaken by what had occurred, telling Bradley over and over that he had not stolen a thing. Bradley had been so concerned with fighting his friend's cause and getting him out from behind bars that he had given very little thought to the bizarre nature in which Roger had been imprisoned.

Now that he thought of it, the fact that his friend had been arrested while out walking the streets of Paris had been strange indeed. Regardless, Bradley managed to have Roger released from prison, although they had been strictly instructed to remain in Paris until matters were settled within the courts – but Bradley had insisted that they leave at once.

He and Roger managed to make their way to England's shores without too much difficulty and relief had filled them as they'd begun their ride back to London. That reprieve had been shattered in an instant when Roger had been thrown backward as a bullet struck him in the chest.

The servants continued to clean the wound the best they could, and soon there was a large pile of bloody bandages in the corner of the room. Bradley paced back and forth in front of the window. It felt like they had been here forever, although truly it had not been that long.

"Where is the doctor?" he inquired. "And where did Barre disappear to? We need him!"

"Your grace," one of the valets spoke up. "The duke's fiancée called him and he went to assist her momentarily. He should return at any moment."

Bradley nodded and resumed pacing.

The physician finally did appear, and it took no more than a quick look at Roger before he turned to Bradley and slowly shook his head. "There's nothing I can do."

He realized that he had, deep within him, known the truth, but still despair ripped through him at the plight of his old friend.

He sat by him all night, praying for life to return to his body. But the physician had been right. Come morning, Roger took his last breath.

## CHAPTER 1

"Stop! No!"

Bradley Hainsworth, Duke of Carrington, woke with a start, hearing his words echoing around the room. Breathing heavily, he stared at the fire in the grate, trying his best to calm his frantically beating heart.

"It was just a dream," he muttered to himself, passing a hand over his face and feeling the sweat on his brow. His skin was gooseflesh, his breathing ragged. "It was just a dream."

However, the truth was that it was not just a dream. It was a memory that refused to leave him. It was there every night, each time his head touched the pillow, repeating itself over and over again.

Roger was dead.

Bradley could still hear the gunshot, could still see the blood-soaked shirt as his friend took his last breath. The blame for all of it sat firmly on his shoulders.

Rubbing one hand down his face, Bradley pushed back the covers, made his way to the window and threw open the drapes, drinking in the early morning light. He could not go back to sleep now, not when the memories of his friend continued to haunt him.

"I will find the man responsible," he bit out, his breath steaming up the glass in the window. "I swear to you, Roger, justice will be done."

Leaning his head against the cool glass, Bradley closed his eyes for a moment, feeling the heavy burden of duty once more roll onto his shoulders. It was not he who had shot Roger, although he could understand why it certainly looked that way. After all, it had only been he and Roger on the road back to London.

Groaning to himself, Bradley left the window in order to ring the bell. It was early yet, but he needed something in his belly and certainly some coffee if he was not to spend the entire day yawning.

Unfortunately, he had a ball to attend the coming evening, which meant that he would have to go through the motions of preparing for such an event while agonizing through it as well.

It was not that he didn't appreciate the invitation, only that he knew that his title and the fact that he remained unattached were the sole reasons for him to garner so much attention from the rest of society. Doubtless, there would be various ladies with their eyes on him, and he would be introduced to countless debutantes with their fawning mamas behind them.

No one cared for *him*, they only cared about his title and his wealth. Most men seemed amenable to finding themselves in such a situation, for they quite enjoyed the attention regardless of its source, but he could not confess the same.

The more they tried to cling to him, the more he withdrew, but that did not mean they relented. It was as if they saw him as a challenge, like it was all a game. They wanted to see which of them would claim his attentions, and then all of society would be abuzz with the news.

Sighing heavily, Bradley walked over to the fire, finding the room a little chilly. The maid would be in shortly to stoke it, but there was no reason he couldn't do such a thing himself.

Adding a few logs and some coal to the grate, he watched in satisfaction as the flames caught almost at once, bringing a wave of heat toward him. Tugging a blanket from his bed, he swung it around himself, fully aware that he now looked like something of a wraith. There would be no more sleep for him tonight.

At that very moment, the door opened and a pale-faced maid poked her head in, apparently surprised to see him awake so early.

"Your grace," she stammered, not quite looking at him. "I have your breakfast tray."

"Enter," he muttered, and the maid did as he bid before placing the tray down by the fire, her eyes darting around the room.

"Send the valet up in about half an hour, will you please?" Bradley asked, dismissing her. The aroma of freshly buttered toast and hot coffee was already making his stomach growl, and as soon as the door closed, he sat down at once and began to eat.

As he did, he began to mentally prepare for the ball that night. For there was only one reason he was attending. It was the only reason he did much of anything most days.

To search out Roger's killer.

\* \* \*

"Are you sure you're ready for this?"

Bradley let out a breath, sending his friend a wry grin in

response to his question. Alastair sat slouched in an upholstered chair across the room, one foot swinging lazily over the arm. He had grown tired of waiting for Bradley downstairs, and so had come to determine what was taking so long.

Bradley was stalling, as always, putting off their inevitable entrance to the ball. "Can you tell just how much I am looking forward to this evening's entertainment?" Bradley asked wryly.

Alistair, Earl of Kenley, was always up for a social event, and he shot him a sharp look. "You don't look particularly convincing, Carrington."

Taking another deep breath, Bradley tried to settle his shoulders, pushing away the tension weighing them down. He was grateful that Alastair had been willing to come to London to assist him, glad that he had at least one more friend he could rely on. Of course, it had meant telling Alastair everything but, once all had been revealed, Alastair had been just as keen as he was to unmask Roger's killer.

"It may be dangerous," Bradley had warned, to which Alastair only laughed.

"It is not as though I am so tied up in business that I cannot spare a few weeks," Alastair had replied, shaking his head at Bradley. "Come now, do not worry about me. You are quite right to decide that you cannot face this alone. I am determined to help you."

"It is just as well," Bradley muttered regarding his thoughts on the evening's entertainment, as he took one final look at his cravat. "It seems I am something of a bore these days and no one else wants to particularly keep me company."

Alastair chuckled. "You've always been a bore, Carrington, but I believe it suits you. There is a certain dignity about you that draws the ladies to you regardless of how grumpy you look."

Rolling his eyes, Bradley sighed dramatically. "It is my curse to bear."

"If you were only not so handsome," Alastair sighed, shaking his head in mock envy at his friend's dark good looks, although his own striking face and blond curls were equally as pleasing to the ladies. "Or if you did not bear such a high title, then I am quite sure no one would be interested in you."

Bradley could not help but chuckle. "How unfortunate for me, indeed."

"Have you actually any intention of taking a wife?"

The serious question caused Bradley to frown. "No, not in the least, at the moment, although it does not stop the grasping mamas from sending their daughters toward me."

"You are going to have to marry at some point."

Bradley grimaced. "Yes, I am fully aware of that, but I feel as though I cannot allow myself to think of it until Roger's killer is brought to justice." He could feel Alastair's eyes on him, and hoped his friend understood. It was a blessing that Alastair had offered to assist him in looking into the matter, when, in truth, Bradley had very few close friends and even fewer that he could be entirely honest with.

"I understand," Alastair said, slowly. "Then I shall simply have to do your share of dancing as well as my own."

Relieved that the atmosphere lightened once again, Bradley chuckled. Alastair was irresistible to the women. Bradley thought that it must have something to do with Alastair's ability to put almost everyone at ease and say the exact words every lady wanted to hear, accompanied by that charming grin of his.

"Very good, Kenley," he muttered, finally satisfied with the state of his cravat. "Come then, we should go."

## CHAPTER 2

"Now, remember to smile."

Isabella Marriott tried not to roll her eyes, well aware of what was expected of her at the ball.

"Gerard, you do not need to coach me on how to behave within society. You might recall that I am from this country, even if you are not."

The grip on her arm tightened painfully, making her aware that her stepbrother was not particularly happy about what she had said. Isabella, however, was not perturbed, having endured such things from him for a good many years.

"You do not have to squeeze my arm so," she continued, calmly. "The fact is, Gerard, I am English and you are French. If anyone is to talk about how to behave at a ball, it should be me."

"I need no instruction," Gerard growled, his grey eyes glinting as he glared at her. "Two years we have lived here, Isabella, and I expect nothing but propriety from you."

Wanting to mention that he had never experienced anything *other* than propriety from her, Isabella wisely chose to keep her mouth closed but wrenched her arm from his grip regardless. Gerard had never been a kind man and had used almost everything he could think of to have her do what he wanted of her. However, although Isabella agreed to some of his requests in order to keep the peace, of late they had become a little more perturbing and she had often refused to do what he had asked.

He had become rather angry at her constant refusals but had been forced to back down, aware that she was not entirely under his control. Yet, Isabella was always on her guard, aware that if she pushed Gerard too far, he could erupt. She had seen the murderous glint in his eye on too many occasions, which rippled a coil of fear through her soul.

The only thing that saved her was the knowledge that, if anything happened to her, the fortune she was to come into would not be handed over to Gerard, but would go to some distant cousin. She realized that Gerard felt it was in his best interests to keep her close, although she was not quite sure why he had always seemed so keen for her to wed. She had to confess that the idea of finding a husband to escape Gerard often crossed her mind.

Walking into the ornate ballroom with its shimmering glass chandeliers imported from Venice, Isabella watched Gerard hurry away from her side almost at once, leaving her quite alone. She wore a white gown with red trim that was simple, yet becoming. She loved the delicate embroidered flowers above the ruffled bottom of the skirt, and the short puff sleeves lined with red lace. As she normally did, Isabella found herself a seat in the quietest area of the ballroom, hoping she would blend into the shadows and remain almost entirely unnoticed. She did not want her brother to see her and demand that she dance with his choice of eligible gentlemen, each of whom would look at her with greed in their eyes.

That was one of the difficulties that came with being a woman of means. Gentlemen did not care for her heart, nor her thoughts or interests. They wanted her fortune, and that was all. The last thing Isabella wanted to do was find herself in a marriage to a man exactly the same as Gerard. It was too bad, for she actually quite loved to dance for the dancing itself, not the men partnered with her.

Isabella smiled as a few of the young ladies made their way past her, and she stood to converse with them for a few minutes. It seemed she was well enough liked by other young women in society, probably because she didn't appear to be much of a threat.

After her return from France, she had at first been looked upon with some animosity. She didn't, however, push herself on any of the young men, nor have a mother to do it for her, which resulted in her getting lost among the many others vying for the attentions of the gentlemen. Soon enough, she was included in polite conversation.

As she listened to the words of gossip floating around her ears, Isabella grew distant as she thought about the last time she had been without any worry, without any kind of cares.

At the same time, she had been quite unaware that her father, Viscount Marriott, was on the verge of ruining all of his business interests in England, and she had thrown herself headlong into all that society had to offer. At just fifteen, she had made her come out a little early, but, regardless, she still had been readily accepted by society. Without a mother to guide her, it had been a difficult experience at times, but she had made the best of it.

Within a few months, however, her father had moved them to France and Isabella had been forced to start life all over again in a country she knew very little about. Her father had eventually met a lady of means and had remarried. Isabella had acquired a stepmother and a stepbrother within a few months. She had never found her stepbrother to be particularly kind, but they had avoided each other for the most part.

Unfortunately for Isabella, life was to take another turn when her father and stepmother had been killed in a tragic carriage accident, along with three others. She had barely accepted her new reality when she discovered that her father had arranged for her to inherit his entire fortune — but for a small stipend for Gerard — although she could only access a part of what he had left her. The rest came to her on the occasion of her marriage. The title and entailed property went to her cousin, but the earned fortune and the English manor near London were hers.

Isabella's musings came to a halt with the arrival of Lady Olivia Jackson. Isabella adored Olivia. Their mothers had been friends as young girls, and when Isabella returned from France, Olivia had been one of the first to welcome her back. They were as different from one another as could be, but perhaps that was why they got along so well.

"Isabella!" cried Olivia as she came over to her. "Why are you hiding in this corner? You're such a wonderful dancer, you should be out on the floor. The dress you are wearing is meant to be seen."

"It's lovely to see you, Olivia," she responded. "Although you know very well I am perfectly content watching the dancers from here."

"I know why you are hiding, and it is not because of the dancers," Olivia said with a frown. "It's because of that boor of a stepbrother of yours. Really, Isabella, I wish you would send him back to France. Does he not have enough to live off from what his mother and your father left for him?"

"It seems not," said Isabella, with a shake of her head. "He seems quite intent on remaining in England."

"And close to you as he wants any money you do have,"

said Olivia with a snort. "Thank goodness you've at least refused to give him any."

Isabella had left France over two years prior as she was determined to escape from the clutches of her stepbrother and evade being trapped by the war. She had made arrangements to return to her family home in England, through her father's faithful steward, and so had left without telling Gerard. The monies she had access to were not of a large amount, but she had lived quietly for three months.

Isabella had very much enjoyed returning to the small estate that had been her childhood home. The furnishings had been sparse, but with careful accounting, Isabella had been able to purchase what she needed. Her father's steward had supplied her with a small staff, and Isabella, once settled, had lived quietly, simply enjoying the freedom she had been blessed with.

Until Gerard.

Isabella listened to Olivia chatter, until the next dance began and Olivia left to find her partner — at every ball she ensured her dance card was always full. Isabella resumed her seat as her eyes roved around the ballroom. She tried to focus on happier times and of happier things.

There were a great many guests, and it was something of a crush already. She chuckled as she saw one of the mothers pulling out her fan, clearly declaring to all who would pay her any attention that she was about to faint. It did not take long for the hosts to take note and, within minutes, the French doors were thrown open and a welcome burst of cool air floated over Isabella.

And still, the guests continued to arrive.

Watching them idly, Isabella felt herself somewhat arrested by the presence of two particular gentlemen descending the stairs. They were both very finely dressed, but it was the expression on their faces that caught her notice most of all. The blond man was grinning broadly, gesturing to a group of gentlemen and ladies that he was, evidently, keen to join, whereas the second man held something of a stern expression.

She watched him closely, not quite certain why she was so drawn to him. Well, perhaps she knew part of the reason. He was one of the most handsome men she had ever seen — dark haired, with a tall, strong frame and a firm jaw to match. But did he never smile? Most of the guests were laughing and talking, but he seemed lost in thought, in whatever serious considerations were running through his mind. Even when his friend left his side, the gentleman stood alone and quiet, moving away from the other guests as his gaze took in the room.

There was a sternness about his expression that made her heart squeeze in sympathy for him. Had he gone through some kind of tragedy? Or was he the kind of gentleman who simply did not enjoy such things as a ball? Or did he not belong here?

She laughed quietly at her silly musings, shaking her head. He was wealthy, of course, given that his clothes were of the highest quality, which meant that there would be a great many ladies seeking his acquaintance.

Perhaps that was why he did not look particularly pleased, although men of that ilk were few and far between. She had always thought that gentlemen appreciated being fawned over, but perhaps this man, whatever his name and title, was the exception. How had she never noticed him before?

Dragging her attention away from him, Isabella tried to concentrate on the other guests, but could not stop herself from flickering her gaze back to the gentleman in question, only to discover that he was gone.

"Ah, Miss Marriott."

Seeing Lord Charles Belrose approach, Isabella inwardly cringed, but rose at once, putting a smile on her face that she did not truly feel. Lord Belrose was one of the many gentlemen that Gerard had introduced to her and, while he was not an unkind man, Isabella simply was not interested in him. However, he appeared quite determined to further their acquaintance, even though Isabella had not given him the slightest bit of encouragement.

"I see that you are sitting here all alone, and that cannot be a good thing!" Lord Belrose said, smiling broadly as his fair hair flopped over his forehead. "Come now, you *must* dance!"

Isabella held out her dance card, sighing inwardly. "Have you spoken to Gerard, Lord Belrose?"

"Indeed," he grinned, with a somewhat boyish look on his face. "It was he who alerted me to your plight!"

She frowned. "Plight?"

"Yes, of sitting here alone, out of sight of all the amiable gentlemen who might wish to dance with you," he exclaimed, looking at her as though she had unknowingly put herself into such a situation. "Come now, let us dance."

Isabella bit back her retort and allowed him to lead her onto the floor, hating that Gerard was, once more, trying to push his influence on her.

She smiled at Belrose, who made a few statements about the weather and their hosts, but then seemed quite unsure of what else to speak with her about. Isabella pitied him, but truly they simply had nothing to discuss. He pasted a simple grin of his own on his face, and as he led her around the dance floor in silence, her mind began to wander.

One day, completely by surprise, her stepbrother had appeared on her doorstep and she had been unable to remove him. Declaring himself determined to look out for his sister, for that was apparently how he thought of her, he had invaded her home and her privacy. He had tried to take over her life, choosing to dominate her existence in whatever way he could and she continually had to fight to prevent him from ruling her. It was exhausting and she had no one to assist her, for who exactly could she turn to? There were no other relatives to speak of. He had come to England to live with her, apparently in order to find a wife of his own, but in two years, she had never seen any singular interest from him in that regard. He seemed much more intent on adding to his coffers and ensuring that the gentlemen of his acquaintance knew that he was not to be trifled with.

Isabella had always known that Gerard had a cruel side, but had soon come to see the full extent of it. He cheated at cards, stole from whomever he chose and, should anyone put up any kind of complaint, he had brute force to prevent them from saying anything more. No one stood in his way. Her staff shrank before him, hardly daring to breathe whenever they were in his presence. In addition, he continually insisted that Isabella had no choice but to marry, and he was taking her father's place in assisting her.

She was quite sure that Gerard wanted her fortune for his own, although she was unsure how he intended to go about getting it.

She continued to run her household as she saw fit, refusing to buy the most expensive cuts of meat or latest styles of furniture that Gerard demanded and, up until now, he had never once struck her for refusing to do as he asked, though he had threatened now and again.

Now he had been more and more adamant that she find a man to marry, and he seemed particularly focused on Lord Belrose. She figured he was trying to get her out of the house so he could keep it for himself, although without her inheritance, she wasn't sure where he would find the funds for the upkeep.

Out of the corner of her eye, she saw Gerard trying to become acquainted with a small group of young ladies, but they seemed to be doing their best to avoid him. As a Frenchman without English property or title, he wasn't much of a catch. He was handsome enough, but the cruel twist to his smile along with his air of self-righteousness turned off most English mamas and daughters.

Which was why he was focused on her prospects instead, thought Isabella as she turned back to Lord Belrose. When the dance came to an end, he began to ask for another, but she made a polite excuse to retreat from the dance floor before he could complete the sentence. Grabbing a glass of champagne, she made her way back to her corner, being sure to find deeper shadows this time.

## CHAPTER 3

Bradley and Alastair entered the ballroom together, having made their way to Lord and Lady Fitzgerald's home without incident. This was the debut ball of the Fitzgeralds' daughter, Lady Lydia, and, as she came from a titled and wealthy family, Bradley was quite sure that she would find herself a suitable husband within a sennight.

Joining the long line of guests, Bradley waited in silence until he was introduced to the lady in question, having first greeted her mother and father. He ignored the faint blush on the girl's cheeks and was nothing but respectful, moving away as quickly as he could.

"I do believe that Lady Lydia has her eye on you," Alastair muttered out of the corner of his mouth as they moved away.

Aware that Lady Lydia and her mother had been scrutinizing him, Bradley shook his head and laughed. "I am not interested. Besides, I am a good twelve years the girl's senior, if not more."

Alastair shrugged. "I doubt that matters. There have been marriages with a greater age difference before."

"Not for me," Bradley growled, a shudder of revulsion

going through him as he thought of the many older gentlemen who were suddenly engaged to young ladies, some of whom were only just out of the schoolroom it seemed. No, that would not be the trap he would fall into. "If I am to marry – for I doubt I shall remain alone for my entire life – I shall make every endeavor to find a lady similar to me in both age and temperament."

Grinning, Alastair slapped Bradley on the back in a friendly manner. "Of course, I was just ribbing you. Now, if you don't mind, I think I shall find those I am acquainted with and put my name down on some dance cards. After all, I do not intend to spend the entire evening standing by *your* side."

"You will not forget our purpose?"

Alastair shook his head, his grin fading. "No, indeed. How could I? I have the names of the gentlemen you wished me to notice up here." He tapped the side of his head, his gaze measured. "Excuse me."

Bradley watched his friend leave, aware of just how easily Alastair was able to converse with those he was acquainted with, as well as the effortlessness at which he greeted new people. It was not something that Bradley found particularly simple, for his words often came out in a rush, tumbling over one another. It was not that he was nervous about new acquaintances, but rather that his mind was so busy thinking about other things — things that mattered — that he found himself struggling to focus.

Since he had returned from France, his sole focus was justice. Roger had been his closest friend for a great many years. They had spent their growing years together at Eton and had talked and joked about finding a suitable wife for one another. Roger had been like a brother, and his loss had left a large hole in Bradley's life. If only they had never become mixed up in the whole France business, then none of this might have happened.

Knowing that it was unwise to start considering all of his regrets, Bradley shook his head and tried not to allow himself to retreat to the decisions of the past. He had made his choice, and with that had come some deal of danger but, then again, that was exactly what he had been looking for. Roger had not been involved at first, but had known of Bradley's activities and was always interested in the goings on. Perhaps, if Bradley had not told him so much about what was happening, then Roger might still be alive.

Frowning to himself, he was pleased to see Lord Rousseau out of the corner of his eye, and he made his way over to speak further with him. He was one of the few Frenchmen here tonight, and often took part in society events.

Bradley knew it had been some time since Rousseau had left France in disgrace, however, so it was unlikely he was the man in question, but it was worth speaking further with him.

Bradley thought back to the journey home with Roger.

Even now, he was not quite sure what had occurred. At times, he thought he could recall another bullet whizz past him as he had reined in his horse, turning back to find his friend, but such had been the fear and horror racing through his veins that he had been unable to think of anything other than getting Roger to safety.

Was it possible that whoever had shot Roger had been aiming for him? Had he been the intended target and Roger simply in the way? Or had the murderer intended to shoot them both?

"It was a setup," Bradley muttered to himself, heaviness filling his soul. "Roger died because of me."

The truth was that had Bradley not chosen to involve himself in the Foreign Office's affairs, then he might now be awakening to a brand-new day with nothing but balls and soirees on his calendar. Together, he and Roger might have gone to White's as they had so often done before. Bradley's choices had led to Roger's death, he was quite sure of it, and the burden of culpability lay heavily on him.

Letting his gaze wander around the room, Bradley knew he had no other choice but to remain here in London and to try and find Roger's killer, the man with links to France. There were a number of gentlemen he wanted to investigate, but nothing concrete, in any respect. At the moment, he was standing in front of a very large wall with no way to overcome it.

The truth was that he could, very easily, put the last few months behind him, find himself a wife, and return to the country, choosing to step away from the Foreign Office and all his involvement with it. That would be the easy option, and certainly one that held a certain measure of appeal.

The weight on his mind had only increased with every passing day, and escaping it all seemed like a very good idea... but Bradley knew that his nightmares would not end until he found Roger's killer.

He reasoned that he had a younger brother, already married and settled, who could take on the title if the worst happened. Having to re-enter the fray of society was not something that brought him any kind of pleasure.

Bradley scowled in annoyance at the thought of dancing all evening. He had to attend such things to continue his surveillance of the *ton*, although now he was looking for someone who had a great deal to hide. Passing information to the French was strictly forbidden, and a man could be hanged for treason if it was discovered.

Seeing Alastair already leading a lady onto the floor, Bradley wondered whether he too should dance straight away, but decided that he would, perhaps initially at least, stay in the corners of the ballroom and simply observe. He did not know which of the suspected men on his list would be present, and it was best that he took some time to study the other guests as unobtrusively as possible. That meant that he would have to find a quiet space where he would not be interrupted.

His gaze was drawn to the darker areas of the ballroom, some hidden entirely in shadow, and it was to one of these corners that he made his way. Walking carefully through the throng of guests, Bradley smiled to himself as the crowd grew less and less congested, until he was finally able to breathe freely. Turning to look behind him, a rush of relief ran through him as he realized just how well hidden he was going to be.

"Oh, excuse me!"

As he had not been paying attention to the path in front of him, Bradley stumbled over something, and, on righting himself, realized that he had practically walked into a young woman who was sitting on a chair, looking up at him with the biggest eyes he had ever seen.

"I do beg your pardon," he muttered, heat rippling up his neck. "I must apologize, I was not looking where I was going."

"Yes," she smiled, apparently quite at ease over what had occurred. "I can see that. Did someone distract you? Or is it that you are trying to hide from a particular lady?"

Warmth infused his cheeks as he cleared his throat, his gaze dancing away from her. "Truthfully, I was simply looking for a place to hide for a time. I have been away from society and this is my first venture since I have returned," he said, with a half-smile. "Even now, I find that not everyone here is favorable company."

His embarrassment lessened as he looked back at her and

saw that her expression was one of sympathy, as if she could easily understand his situation.

"I quite agree," she murmured, softly. "Do not let me keep you from melting into the shadows!"

It was his cue to leave her side but Bradley found his feet quite fixed to the ground, as he was overcome with a strange desire to sit by her. She was quite a beautiful woman, with jet black hair and dark brown eyes that darted from here to there as she watched the other guests. He wondered why she sat here alone.

A certain tension radiated from her, and Bradley saw her shoulders lift a little as she stiffened, her eyes fixed on a certain spot across the room. It took everything in him not to turn around and see who the lady was watching, knowing he would appear quite rude if he did so. Instead, he chose to take a few steps to his left, blocking her view of whomever she was looking at, and, he hoped, hiding her from sight. Bradley smiled as her eyes lifted to his, confusion on her face.

"I know this is quite untoward, given that we have not been introduced," he began, with a slight bow. "But might I sit with you for a few minutes?"

Her smile was immediate. "But of course! I would be glad of your company, Lord...?" Her eyes twinkled and Bradley grew frustrated with himself for, yet again, blundering over the introductions.

"I do apologize. I am the Duke of Carrington." He gave an ornate bow, lifting his head to see her eyes widen just a little.

"Your grace," she stammered, making to get to her feet. "I do apologize for—"

"None of that, I beg you," he interrupted, gesturing for her to sit back down. "I am not a stickler for propriety."

She swallowed, biting her lip for a moment. Bradley found himself filled with an urge to reach forward and brush his finger along her lower lip so that she might free it. The longing was so strange and so strong that Bradley had to clench his hands tightly into fists so as not to move. He had never responded to a lady like this before.

Was it because she had no awareness of his true title and so had spoken to him with candor and a kindness that held no pretense or falsehood? All the ladies he met at balls such as these were far too complimentary of him, practically gushing with pleasure on seeing him and attempting to talk with him about their great many attributes, in the hope that he might think them worthy of being his bride.

"Might I ask your name?" he said, softly, thinking that the pink in her cheeks made her even more appealing.

"I am Miss Isabella Marriott," she said, quietly, lowering her lashes for a moment. "My father was Lord Sunderley."

Bradley frowned. "I do not recall meeting him."

"My father chose to move to France some years ago," she explained. "He married again but, on his death, I returned to England."

At the mention of France, Bradley's ears pricked up, but he dismissed her as a suspect almost at once. There was no earthly way that a woman such as this could be a traitor to the Crown. Besides, the Foreign Office had made it very clear that there were only gentlemen to be watched, and all of them born in France. Clearly, Miss Marriott did not fulfill that requirement.

"Did you miss England?" he asked easily, sitting down next to her.

"Oh, yes, your grace," she replied, earnestly. "I have very much enjoyed being back on England's shores these last couple of years."

"And do you live alone?"

A shadow passed over her face, and, for a moment, her eyes darted to the crowd of guests, before returning to him.

"No, I do not. My stepbrother came to join me a few months after my return."

Bradley lifted his eyebrows. "Your stepbrother?"

"Gerard Durand," she explained, with a tight smile. "He was my stepmother's son. She had lost her own husband some years before, and when my father remarried, he gained both a wife and a stepson."

"And he is here now?"

She nodded, her gaze drifting away. "Yes," she murmured, softly. "He is. He enjoys balls and the like."

"And you do not?" he asked, lightly. "I would have thought that a lady such as yourself would have had her dance card filled almost at once."

A blush filled her cheeks, although her eyes sparkled with delight. "You are very kind, your grace."

He smiled, seeing that she was entirely unused to receiving such compliments. Something about her put him more at ease than he usually found himself at such gatherings. "Might I ask for the honor of dancing with you?"

She looked completely taken aback, although her hand lifted and he was able to reach for her dance card. To his surprise, it was nearly empty. "You truly do wish to hide away, do you not, Miss Marriott?"

He glanced up at her and saw that she opened her mouth as if to explain, only to give a slight shake of her head, closing it again. He filled his name in two places. When her eyes flew up to meet his, a spark flew between them, which seemed to catch her off guard as she quickly looked down.

Bradley knew that it was not like him to look forward to a dance, but he thought dancing was better than hiding here among the wallflowers for the remainder of the evening. Of course, the temptation to sit by Miss Marriott for the next few hours was great indeed, but Bradley knew he could not show her such a great amount of attention. It was bound to be noticed at some point and rumors would fly around the room by the end of the evening. No, he would have to pull himself away from her company, but the promise of two dances with her nearly made up for it.

"I should leave you now," he said, rising from his chair and letting her dance card fall. "I look forward to our first dance, Miss Marriott. Thank you for speaking with me."

"You are very welcome, your grace," she murmured, reading his name on her dance card. Bradley moved back into the throng of guests, quite sure he could feel her eyes on him as he walked away.

## CHAPTER 4

For some time, Isabella was quite overcome with astonishment at what had occurred, hardly believing that she was to dance with a duke – and not only once, but twice. Any woman would find him to be an incredibly attractive man, with dark hair and brilliant blue eyes that always seemed intensely focused – and she had felt a flurry of excitement in her belly when they were focused on her and he had signed his name on her dance card. The way he had smiled at her had sent a warmth to her cheeks, making her feel as though she were the only woman in the room.

She had not intended to dance at all again, after her turn with Lord Belrose, for to do so would have her stepbrother notice her. As had happened before, she would then have to deal with a barrage of questions regarding each and every gentleman, as though Gerard was to decide which of them might be worth pursuing. It did not matter that Isabella had told him repeatedly that she did not wish to marry, for he ignored her completely and was often very insistent that she accept suit from various gentlemen – which, of course, she refused to do.

In addition, he always appeared to be in search of extremely *wealthy* gentlemen for her hand, which Isabella could not understand since she would be bringing a large fortune into the marriage anyway. Gerard confused her greatly, which only added to the fear she had over his determination to rule her life.

Her eyes remained on the duke as he walked away, and excitement rushed through her at the thought of being in his arms. Something about him tugged at her deep inside. Of course, once he discovered the truth about her father and the scandal his failed business had caused, she was quite sure he would want to take himself as far from her as possible.

Never mind that her father had redeemed himself by finding success in France — that would not be known or remembered in England. Besides that, she was a simple viscount's daughter and certainly nowhere near the duke's rank.

She had heard the duke's name being spoken now and again during her time back in society but had never met the man. Remembering how he had said to have just returned to town, Isabella smiled to herself, thinking that it was obvious the man did not want to fling himself, head first, back into all of society's pleasures. There was a certain gravitas about him, as though he was quite determined not to be what society expected.

A duke, after all, could do very little wrong. Even if he were to rob maidens of their innocence, or to take every last penny from a man of lesser title at the card table, society would perhaps shake their heads, but there would be no true shunning. No one would give a duke the cut direct, there would be no penalty for his behaviors — but yet, this one did not seem so inclined.

His eyes had been sharp as they'd studied her, causing her to feel nearly naked before him. He had asked pertinent questions and seemed truly interested in what she had to say. There was no leer on his face, nor any ribald words escaping from his mouth as she had come to expect of some of the more wealthy and titled gentlemen. No, it seemed that this duke was, as far as she could tell, quite the opposite of what society expected of him.

The minutes seemed to take hours as she waited, with a growing impatience, for her first dance with him. She even rose from her seat and walked a little closer to the other guests, only to frantically rush back to her chair, afraid that he would be unable to find her.

*He is not about to turn around and ask you to marry him, Isabella,* she told herself firmly, and her stomach began to swirl with nerves. *Enjoy being in his arms but do not lose yourself in a dream.*

It was not as though Isabella did not have her fair share of suitors, but they had each been introduced to her and then encouraged by her stepbrother and that meant that she disliked them all almost immediately. Those that Gerard did not introduce her to were usually scared away when he made their acquaintance. The fact that this man had asked to dance with her without any kind of encouragement or promises from her stepbrother brought her joy, if nothing else.

"Ah, Miss Marriott. I believe this is our dance. I do hope the rest of your dance card has been filled in my absence."

Isabella did not reply, but simply smiled at him and placed her gloved hand on his as she rose. The duke smiled at her in return and made some comment about the evening having been brightened by her company, which only made the warmth in her heart burst into life. The music began and, realizing that it was to be the waltz, Isabella stepped into his awaiting arms and allowed him to lead her around the floor.

He was a wonderful dancer, moving them effortlessly through the other couples, his steps firm and sure. Isabella lost herself entirely, feeling as though she were in a dream, dancing on clouds.

The duke said very little, though she hoped he was enjoying the moment just as much as she, and was unwilling to break the quietness that surrounded them. Even as the music seemed to fade around them, Isabella looked up at the duke, their gazes locking. She found she could not look away, as she drowned in the depths of his eyes. His hand tightened a fraction on her waist and his breath brushed her cheek. Her eyes fluttered closed as she fought the urge to reach up and kiss him, knowing that she was being utterly ridiculous.

This was a dance. Just like every other dance occurring around them. To him, it was likely a way to pass the time. He could never know that to her, it was everything.

The dance came to an end, and Isabella allowed the duke to lead her from the floor and return her to her seat. His hand clasped hers as he pressed a light kiss onto the back of it, causing her heart to quicken.

"I look forward to our second dance, Miss Marriott," he murmured, quietly. "You are a wonderful dancer."

Isabella tried to find something to say in response, but instead, only managed to smile at him, keeping her composure until he turned his back and walked away from her.

Sagging slightly in her seat, Isabella wished she could fan her face as the heat rose up in her cheeks. She could not stop herself from being overwhelmed, sighing as though she were a maiden in love. It was quite ludicrous to be caught up in feeling over a man after only one dance, but Isabella chose to revel in it instead of pushing it away.

She would allow herself this one delight, this one moment of happiness. Even if she never again cast her eyes upon the duke after this evening, she would always remember the night with fondness. In his arms, all the worries and burdens she carried had slipped away for a moment, giving her a taste of the freedom she had almost forgotten.

Unfortunately, she was brought back to the reality of her situation with the sound of a sharp voice.

Gerard.

"Who was that you were dancing with, Isabella?"

Sighing, Isabella shook her head. "It is not of importance, Gerard."

"Was it not the Duke of Carrington?"

Irritated, Isabella looked up at him. "If you already knew, then why did you ask?"

"I am just surprised to see that he chose to dance with *you*, of all people," Gerard replied, dryly. "Took pity on you, did he?"

Not rising to his taunts, Isabella shrugged. "Something like that." Isabella did not want to show her stepbrother that his words needled her, digging into the doubts she already felt. It had come as something of a surprise to be asked to dance, but perhaps the duke was only making up for practically falling into her lap. Gerard may be cruel, but he was right. There could be no true attraction there, no particular interest on his part. After all, he was a duke and could dance with anyone – and court anyone – he chose.

Isabella knew that a duke would have to marry well, and usually with a lady who held as high a title as he could find – not exactly a requirement she fulfilled.

Sighing inwardly, Isabella resigned herself to the fact that she would enjoy one more dance with the man, and then their acquaintance would draw to a close. It was what she could expect, given her station, and to have any further hopes was quite ridiculous.

"The Duke of Carrington," Gerard repeated, his eyes

finding the man of Isabella's thoughts once more, who was now dancing with another young lady. Isabella wondered if she was affected as greatly as she had been.

Gerard echoed her thoughts. "What a shame you could not hold his attentions, Isabella, although I should not be surprised at his lack of interest."

"I do believe I have another dance with him," Isabella replied, hotly, hating herself for allowing his harsh words to get under her skin. Looking away, she slammed her mouth closed, refusing to say another word. However, Gerard appeared to be quite delighted with the news, not laughing at her for responding to his jibes as she'd thought.

"You must introduce him to me after your dance, Isabella," he said, putting one hand on her shoulder and squeezing it lightly. "I insist upon it."

He did not give her a chance to argue but instead walked away from her, throwing one more look back over his shoulder before disappearing into the crowd. Isabella shook her head, groaning quietly. If anyone would put the Duke of Carrington off continuing an acquaintance with her, it would be Gerard. Then again, she should have expected as much, given that the duke was both wealthy and titled.

If only she could get away from her stepbrother. She would, once the time came, but she had a task to fulfill first.

She tried not to think about her continued, frantic searches through her father's old things, knowing that there were still a great many rooms to go through. If she could find what she was looking for, then she could be free of Gerard for good, never having to marry as he wished. Her eyes lingered on the dancers, a slight smile spreading across her face at the rainbow of color from the ladies twirling around the floor.

Thankfully, Isabella was not without hope, for she had a plan in mind.

It all came from her dear grandmother, a lady she had known only for a few years when she was a young child. She could still remember how warm and kind she had been, which was, she learned, quite unusual for a grandmama. At times, Isabella was quite sure she could still smell the perfume her grandmother had worn, the scent wrapping itself around her heart and bringing tears to her eyes.

"If you are ever in need," she remembered her grandmother saying, "then look for this book. It will tell you where the treasure is buried."

Of course, at the time, Isabella had no idea of what the old lady was saying, but it had been repeated to her so often that the words had been seared into her mind.

The book was her grandmother's diary. It was small with a brown leather cover and a piece of cord tying it together. It looked quite ordinary, except for the single diamond that had been placed in the center of the cover. Isabella could still recall how it glinted in the sun, sending shards of light everywhere.

"It will tell you where the treasure is buried," Isabella murmured to herself, those words so familiar and yet so frustrating. She had never known what this so-called treasure was, not until her father had taken her to France. She had heard him mutter something about a ruby encrusted jewelry box, which held the Marriott jewelry.

Being as hard up as he was at the time, with business having gone so poorly, he had been searching for it so that he might sell the pieces to bring back some of his lost riches but had been unable to locate the item. When Isabella had asked where it might be, he had, at first, started in surprise that she had heard him talk aloud to himself, before declaring that he had no clue where the piece might be and promptly blaming his deceased mother.

"She must have taken it," he had said, shaking his head.

"She must have put it somewhere that I could never get to it, although I do not know why she would do such a thing."

Isabella bit her lip, recalling how she had not said a single word to her father, although the urge to share her grandmother's secret strengthened the more she watched her father struggle. In the end, however, she had never spoken a word about the connection between her grandmother's diary and the missing heirloom. Her grandmother must have had her reasons for not sharing with her father, and Isabella vowed to do as her grandmother had wished. She held her grandmother's trust close in her heart as a precious gift.

In addition, she had despised the idea of her father selling something that was obviously very precious, realizing that the necklace had meant a great deal to her grandmother. It had proven to be a wise consideration, for while she loathed the idea of selling it herself, she knew her grandmother would understand the freedom that her precious heirloom could bring.

But first, she had to find her grandmother's diary, in order to read where she had put the chest and, thus far, Isabella had come up with nothing at all. There was still a great deal of the house to search but the fact that her stepbrother was present with her made the opportunities to look few and far between.

Her eyes caught sight of the duke standing to one side, talking to an acquaintance. She could not help her attraction to him, warmth curling in her belly as she looked at him.

One more dance. One more dream.

Then she would return to the truth of her life.

## CHAPTER 5

Bradley had been quite looking forward to his next dance with the beautiful young woman he had been so drawn to. She was not like the other ladies he was acquainted with, who were either thrust upon him by their mothers or threw themselves at him on their own. This woman was quiet, reserved, and yet an inner strength radiated from her.

She was all smiles and politeness as she danced with him once more, though he could sense the tension growing in the slight, shapely frame under his hands and he was overwhelmed by the urge to draw her close and keep her safe – though from what, he had no idea, and nor was it his place to ask. When the dance ended and he led her off the floor, he saw her head whip from one side to the other, as if looking for someone.

"Is everything all right, Miss —"

"Yes, of course," she responded in rush, taking a step away as if she wanted to be rid of him. "Thank you so much for the lovely dances, your grace."

She turned to leave but was suddenly blocked by a large

body. Bradley stepped forward to defend her, but it seemed she knew the man.

"Ah, my dear Isabella," the man said to her as she seemed to shrink away from him. "You must introduce me to your new friend." The smile on his face as he looked down at her had a sinister twist to it, making even Bradley shiver.

"Of course, Gerard," she said, biting her lip in a way that caused a stir inside him. He noted the animation that had been present on her face and in her countenance as they danced had disappeared, while the tension and sense of unease was heightened.

Who was this man who insisted on an introduction?

She reluctantly held a hand out toward him. "Gerard, may I present the Duke of Carrington? Your grace, this is my stepbrother, Mr. Gerard Durand."

Bradley started at the introduction, his focus shifting from Isabella's beauty to the pair of them standing together. Her brother — stepbrother — was Gerard Durand? This was the very man he had been looking to better acquaint himself with, to determine his recent whereabouts and ties to the situation in France. He took a closer look at Isabella herself. He was attracted to her, yes, but was there any chance that she could be somehow involved in this? He must be careful not to let his desire for her cloud his judgement or become a distraction, though it would not hurt to get closer to her to learn more about her and her stepbrother.

He realized he hadn't said anything, as he took in the faces of the siblings who were waiting for a response.

"Ah, yes, good to meet you, Durand," he said. "Your sister is a wonderful dancer."

Durand nodded. "I'm glad to hear she pleased you," he said, with a smug look on his face. "Should you care for another —"

"Gerard!" she cut him off, her face going very pale as

Bradley couldn't help but raise his eyebrows at the man's forwardness. It seemed that while Miss Marriott was well used to polite society, her stepbrother was not aware of his boundaries.

"It was kind of the duke to dance with me twice already," she continued, a hand on Durand's arm as if she were trying to move him to continue on his way, but he would not budge. "Your grace, I appreciate the dances and I do so hope you enjoy your evening."

"It was my pleasure," he said, trying to find Isabella's eyes once again, but her face remained downcast. "Durand, you are French? How long have you been in England?"

"Indeed, I am French, but I have been here about two years now," the man replied. "Of course I miss my country, but it is much more important to be here to look after Isabella, now that her father has passed."

Bradley didn't miss the look Isabella gave him from the corner of her eye, but it was gone as quickly as he had noticed it, her face froze in a polite smile once again.

"And do you return often to visit?" he asked.

"Not for some time," Durand responded, though it piqued Bradley's interest to find out when exactly he had last been in the country. As he tried to think of a way to further question Durand, the man himself provided him with the opportunity.

"I say, Carrington, we are having a house party in a week's time just outside of London. We would love to have you join us."

"A house party?" Isabella looked at him, aghast.

"Of course! Belrose will be there, as will Rousseau and a few others of course. Come, join us!"

"I would be delighted," Bradley heard himself saying, before requesting an invitation for the Earl of Kenley as well.

It would be nearly a week of time he could spend learning more of the two Frenchman and Belrose, a man of French ancestry. All he had to do was keep Miss Marriott from continuing to enchant him over his stay.

He snuck another glance at her, seeing her long lashes hide what he knew to be warm brown eyes. That, he realized, may prove to be the most difficult part of his plan.

* * *

Isabella's face was flaming as she finally extricated herself from the situation. She should not have excused herself from a duke, but she couldn't listen to another word between them as she feared what would come out of Gerard's mouth. It had gone just as poorly as she had imagined, which was why she had tried to prevent it in the first place. Gerard had no manners whatsoever, and she had seen the duke's varied horrified expressions throughout the course of the conversation.

"Isabella!" She heard her name being hissed in delight by Olivia as she joined her. "Do you know who that was? You were dancing with the Duke of Carrington — twice! All the young ladies have been longing to dance with him tonight, and you were the first he chose!"

Isabella turned to Olivia.

"I believe he just took pity on me and was being kind," she said. "And now that he's met Gerard…. Oh, Olivia, Gerard told him we were having a house party next week! Can you believe it? I must not only begin planning, but funding the thing, and inviting guests…. I would cancel it altogether, had he not invited a duke. There is no plausible way I could prevent this now. Why the duke accepted, heaven only knows. I could tell he had been put off by the conversation with Gerard, yet he still said yes. Oh, say you'll come and make things bearable."

"Oh but of course!" Olivia squealed with delight. "This is actually quite wonderful. The duke must want more time with you. *That* is why he's attending, I am sure of it. There is no question that Mother will be interested, and I will arrive early to help you prepare."

"Thank you, Olivia," said Isabella gratefully. "I can always count on you."

"Of course."

Isabella trusted Olivia, but had not told her of the diary or treasure. She was a good friend, but sometimes had difficulty remembering when to hold her tongue. Isabella was disappointed as a houseful of guests would make it quite difficult to continue her search of many of the outbuildings or bedrooms throughout the manor. She would have to take extra precautions to ensure she wasn't caught sneaking around.

The fact she had to hide her actions in her own house was unbelievable, but such was the importance of keeping her intentions away from Gerard.

She was forced to admit, however, that a small part of her was secretly thrilled at Gerard's impulsive invitation, as it would provide her the opportunity to spend more time with the duke. She knew she was being foolish, but if she could continue having half as interesting conversations with him as they had on the dance floor, she would soon fall madly in love. He had conversed with intelligence, and had not spoken down to her or discounted any of her thoughts. His blue eyes had pierced into hers as he had held her gaze. She had seen the way he looked at her change after the introduction to Gerard, and she inwardly cursed her stepbrother for putting a stain on her. She had to rid herself of him, of this life.

With renewed focus on finding the diary and therefore

the treasure chest, she said goodnight to Olivia and made her way out of the ballroom and to the carriage.

She had to begin preparing for this blasted house party of Gerard's.

And to steel her heart against a certain duke.

## CHAPTER 6

"Remind me where is it we are going?"

Bradley chuckled. "To the Marriott estate."

"For a house party?"

Nodding, Bradley tried not to roll his eyes at his friend. "Really, Kenley, you did not have to consume *quite* so much brandy last evening, even if it is the finest in all of England."

Alastair did not reply but groaned as the carriage hit a slight bump, jostling the two men. They had attended a game of billiards, and Alastair had too good of a time, as he was wont to do.

"We are going because Gerard Durand is one of the Frenchmen I wish to investigate," Bradley continued, reminding Alastair of what he had previously explained. Apparently, Alastair had been too much in his cups to pay attention when Bradley had explained the situation to him, meaning that they had to go over each detail again. "Durand was very keen to meet me at the ball last week and, when he invited me to his house party, I simply had to accept."

"And you insisted on dragging me along as well," Alastair muttered, his eyes still closed.

"Of course," Bradley agreed. "I need someone to keep an eye on Durand while I search the premises."

Alastair drew in a long breath, before cracking open one eye. "You think you will find something?"

Bradley shrugged. "I might. As I said, there are a few gentlemen of interest and Durand is one of them. However, he has also included in his house party Lord Rousseau and Lord Belrose who, if you recall, have long-standing connections to France."

"Belrose's great-grandmother, was it not?"

"Indeed it was," Bradley said. "See, you did remember something after all. I do believe that Belrose has strong family connections to his relatives who reside there, which might make him a suspect in the whole, sordid affair." The corner of his mouth tipped up into a wry smile. "Besides, it may turn out that Durand is the man I have been searching for, especially if he tries to do away with me."

Alastair frowned. "That is not funny, Carrington."

Bradley shrugged. "It is the truth, though, is it not?"

Letting out an exasperated sigh, Alastair shook his head. "The man might just be keen to have you present around his sister," he said, quietly. "I was not the only one who noticed you dancing with her – twice."

"That is not the reason I accepted Durand's late invitation," Bradley protested at once with a shake of his head. "She is amiable, of course, and I was delighted to have the opportunity to dance with her, but it was only because I wanted to know more about her brother. How better to gain an introduction than through the woman? No one would suspect a thing." He smiled grimly. "And I was successful in my endeavors, was I not?"

Alastair gave him a sharp, assessing look, before tipping his hat over his eyes and resting his head back against the squabs. He remained so for the rest of the journey, giving Bradley more than enough time to think.

The truth was that he *did* find Miss Marriott a very appealing young lady, although he would never admit that she was one of the reasons he had accepted Durand's invitation to his house party. Durand was a man worth looking into, and perhaps Bradley's ongoing acquaintance with his sister might lead to some kind of revelations about the gentleman in question.

Miss Marriott had not seemed altogether pleased with introducing them to one another. Her gaze had been measured, but there had been a tightness about her mouth that betrayed the tension she felt. Why she would feel so, he did not know, but there was something about their relationship that gave him cause for concern. Miss Marriott had been a delight to dance with and to talk to, but she had completely disappeared when in the presence of her stepbrother. Was she afraid of him? Worried about what he might say or do?

Realizing that he was slowly losing a hold of what was truly important, Bradley attempted to remove his thoughts from Miss Marriott, surprised at how difficult he found it. He could still see her laughing eyes, which held depths that he wanted to explore, her pert lips that had been almost begging to be kissed.

However, Bradley would not allow himself to trifle with her. Not only must he put up his guard in case she had anything to do with the ploys of the Frenchmen, he was not currently interested in matrimony.

Solving Roger's death came first, which meant that everything else took second place. He would not toy with the lady, as much as he wanted to, and of course he had no time for anything beyond a flirtation.

Perhaps, once the killer had been unmasked, he might

return to her with true intentions of discovering if they might suit, but, for now, he would keep himself entirely focused on the task at hand. Miss Marriott was a distraction that he could not allow himself to be caught up in. His thoughts were already overrun by her from two dances — this would not do.

Giving himself a stern talking too, Bradley reminded himself that he needed to focus entirely on Gerard Durand, as well as the two other French gentlemen who would be in residence. He had no idea who the other guests were to be, for Durand had been a little scarce on details, but, for the moment, that did not matter. He would settle himself in, and appear as happy and as unconcerned as any guest might be. However, he would always keep his eyes sharp, his ears listening for any spoken French. Alastair would be there to help him when it came time to search the man's home, in the hope that he might find some kind of incriminating evidence.

Whether he found anything or not, Bradley was determined to look carefully and methodically, so that he could leave the estate with either an assurance of Durand's loyalty to the Crown, or evidence of his treason.

\* \* \*

THEIR ARRIVAL WENT SMOOTHLY, with Gerard Durand standing at the front door to welcome them both. The manor was modest but well kept, and Bradley admired the beautiful gardens that began in front and swept around the back of the house. He and Alastair were shown to their rooms, and left alone for a few hours to rest, a tray sent to each of them.

Bradley, having changed and enjoyed a leisurely respite in front of the roaring fire in his charmingly decorated bedchamber, sent both Durand's maid and his own valet away, telling them that they would not be required again until the morning. Bradley was more than able to look after himself when it came to retiring, although he could tell that his valet was a little concerned about the state of Bradley's clothing come the next day.

His eyes roving around the room, Bradley spotted a small door to the left of the large wardrobe. Wondering if it was his dressing room, he turned the handle, which opened at once. Sticking his head in, he saw a small room with another door just across from him.

"So it is a dressing room," he said to himself, wondering why his valet had not seen fit to use it. Perhaps he had simply assumed that the door had been locked. Bradley would have to tell him about it in the morning. However, his gaze was caught by some old trunks in the corner, as well as one large wardrobe. Were there clothes within? Bradley decided that his valet would be the one to complete the exploration of the small room, for he quite fancied another of the small cakes waiting for him by the fire.

He was just about to step back inside, when the door opposite him turned, and, much to his surprise, he found himself staring into the face of a confused, and suddenly obviously embarrassed, Miss Marriott.

"Oh, my goodness!" she exclaimed, her face burning with color. "I am terribly sorry, your grace. I did not realize my brother had...." Her hand covered her mouth, her words trailing off.

Bradley shook his head and tried to smile, wondering what on earth Gerard Durand was playing at, placing him in a room opposite Miss Marriott. He *did* appreciate the opportunity to see her again. She was wearing a simple blue dress, which, along with the braided hair that hung in front of one shoulder, softened her look and heightened the beauty of her face, with its high cheekbones and warm brown eyes.

ONCE UPON A DUKE'S DREAM

"My apologies, Miss Marriott. I am quite sure this door should have been locked and it was my own inquisitiveness that pushed me to open it. I shall ensure not to venture in here for the duration of my stay. Please, forgive me."

She shook her head, her hand dropping to her side as she averted her eyes, apparently unable to look directly at him.

"Only..." he noticed her hand curling into a fist of frustration. "My stepbrother can, at times, do such things as this on purpose and, should anyone discover it, he will place the blame on my staff and punish them without a moment's hesitation. I have my own set of house keys below stairs and will ensure your door is locked by this evening."

Bradley opened his door a little wider, although he did not step inside. Leaning against the doorframe, he looked at her steadily, hoping his words came across casually. "This is your home, then?"

She frowned. "I beg your pardon?"

"You said that they were your staff," he explained, with a soft smile, hoping he might get some more information about Gerard out of her. "I thought this was your brother's estate."

He was surprised at her most unladylike snort of derision, as well as the anger that jumped into her expression.

"No, your grace," she replied, tersely. "This is my home, not my *step*brother's. My father's will made it mine and mine alone." Her expression took on something of a distant look as she lost herself in memories. "He must have taken a great deal of time to ensure that I was his beneficiary, for I have heard it can be difficult for women to inherit."

Bradley smiled at her, thinking that even in her anger and state of undress she was quite lovely. The way her eyes flashed added to the intensity of her gaze.

"Your stepbrother is only here until you decide his time is

at an end, then?" he asked, softly. "He does not intend to reside here long, I would imagine."

Miss Marriott's eyes jumped back to his and she folded her arms across her chest, looking suddenly wary. "Gerard has lived with me for almost two years," she said slowly. "He insists he is intent on finding an English wife, and I believe he intends to make this place his home."

"His home?" Bradley repeated, his smile gone. "But this is your home, Miss Marriott."

She lifted one delicate shoulder but did not say more, though Bradley caught the resolved look on her face. It seemed she had plans of her own, although she was not forthcoming of them.

"I presume he then must conduct all his affairs from here?" Bradley asked, hoping that she would not find his question too impertinent. "Or does he have a place of his own?"

Miss Marriott studied him for a moment before answering. "My father's study has now become my stepbrother's," she said, slowly. "However, should you have any questions regarding this place and its profits, I beg you to ask such questions of me rather than Gerard. I keep my own steward, who has been with this house for decades. He is loyal to me, and I know all the goings on of my property."

She lifted her chin, as though defying him to think less of her for doing so, but Bradley could only stare at her in admiration. Miss Marriott was an intelligent lady, as well as quick-witted, which only added to his respect for her character.

"I think nothing ill of you, Miss Marriott," he murmured, feeling a slight stirring in his heart as well as his loins. "Thank you for answering my questions. I hope you do not think me impertinent for doing so."

The defiance in her eyes faded away and her arms

dropped to her sides once again. "No, not in the least," she murmured, quietly. "I should return to my room. I look forward to seeing you at dinner."

She lingered, not shutting the door as she waited for his response. Bradley smiled at her, enjoying the sight of her standing there. The anger in her eyes had sparked a ripple of warmth in her cheeks and, if he was honest, he found her completely breathtaking. A small strand of dark hair was loose from her braid and hung against her cheek. Bradley had to stop himself from leaning forward and brushing it behind her ear, wondering what it might feel like between his fingers.

Her skin was alabaster, smooth and unblemished, her wide eyes hiding a great many emotions. He longed to see her smile, unhindered by fear or anxiety, her mouth curving gently. Allowing his eyes to discreetly run down the length of her frame, he took in her soft curves and the gentle swell of her breasts. What a beauty she was.

Suddenly aware of his body's reaction to her, and quite astonished by the swiftness of it, he cleared his throat and gave her a quick bow.

"Until we meet again," Bradley repeated, waiting until she had closed the door before pushing himself away from the doorframe and shutting his. Leaning against it for a moment, he took a deep breath, cursing himself for how utterly captivated he found Miss Marriott.

"But there is more to Gerard Durand than meets the eye," he muttered to himself, walking back to the fire and seating himself in front of it once more. Clearly, he had been given one of the best bedchambers of the home, with its flowing forest-green draperies, gold walls, and beautifully painted landscapes that hung around the room. How interesting it was adjoining Miss Marriott's. "Has Durand taken over Miss Marriott's home? Her life?" There was certainly some kind of discord in their relationship, shown by the upset and anger in her face when she had explained to Bradley that this was, in fact, her home and not her stepbrother's.

"This shall be a very interesting week," Bradley said aloud, pouring himself a small brandy, as he tried to brush away the thought of Miss Marriott through the unlocked doors, and focus instead on his task at hand. "A very interesting week, indeed."

# CHAPTER 7

Isabella found herself once again dressing carefully for dinner the next evening after spending the day watching the duke. She had few opportunities to speak with him the past evening, and the men spent most of the day hunting while she entertained the women inside. Tonight she carefully chose a beautiful lavender gown, with cap sleeves and a high waist. Her maid artfully arranged her hair pulled back away from her face, but for a couple of curls to hang down over her sculpted cheekbones.

She told herself she was being silly. A duke would not be interested in a girl like her, and if he was, it was not anything serious. She may be a bit of fun, but that was it. She was the daughter of a mere viscount, and one that had been scandalized in England. Not only that, her stepbrother was French, and his demeanor cast a pall over the family. Why the duke had even agreed to come to this house party, she didn't know, but she continued to tell herself that just because he was here did not mean he had the slightest interest in anything regarding her.

How awful of Gerard to put the duke in the adjoining room with the doors unlocked. Isabella kept the room for the lady of the home for herself, but was careful to always lock the door to the master's suite. What was Gerard playing at? She had been humiliated to open the door to find the duke standing there. The man now likely thought she was duke-hunting at this party.

Isabella's heart fluttered a bit as she stepped into the drawing room. She had taken longer than she had planned on preparing herself, and many of the guests were already inside. She saw Gerard holding court with the Duke of Carrington, Charles Belrose, and Lady Lydia Fitzgerald. Upon leaving the ball last week, Gerard had invited their hosts to this sudden house party. They had been quite reluctant until they heard the Duke of Carrington was attending. That changed their minds completely, and here they were.

Lady Lydia was a pretty little thing. Tiny and blonde, she was young but already knew how to charm a gentleman, looking up at the duke from below long lashes. She pouted at the right moments, smiled when necessary. She may have been young, but she was the type of woman men like the duke were wont to pursue — pretty, of a good family, with all the right connections. Isabella tried to push down the jealousy that rose to the surface of her mind, concentrating instead on keeping Gerard from causing any further embarrassment to their family as she joined their circle of conversation.

"Good evening, Miss Marriott," the duke greeted her with a warm smile on his face before returning to the conversation at hand. The men were talking war, which made Isabella stiffen. Her stepbrother may have been in England for two years, but she knew that despite his outward appearances and the front he put on for other Englishmen, he was French through and through, supportive of the French Emperor and disdainful of the English. Why he remained here in the country he hated, she would never know.

"Did you hear the recent news of Wellington's latest victory?" asked Charles Belrose. "It was in Spain, at Vitoria. He commanded over 80,000 men, taking down the French. He didn't get Bonaparte though — not yet."

The duke nodded. "He will, though. Bonaparte is sure to make an error at some point that will lead to his capture. He is too arrogant, too self-assured. The time will come."

Isabella could see Gerard tense beside her as he struggled not to say anything. He loved the Emperor of France and while he wouldn't sing his praises in this crowd, he also disliked any ill to be spoken of the man. *Please, Gerard*, she prayed. *Keep your mouth shut.*

"He's not so bad," Gerard spoke up, as Isabella sighed to herself. "He's an excellent strategist, and has won many battles and much land for France. You cannot argue that."

"He's aiming to take over the continent, Durand," responded the duke, who seemed strained. "Is this how all of the French feel?"

Gerard bristled, his spine going straight as he realized he had said too much. "I'm not saying he is necessarily in the right in his aims, but he is an intelligent man we should not speak poorly of."

The duke smiled tightly and looked at the women around him. "Perhaps we should save this discussion for after dinner," he said to Gerard and Lord Belrose. "I don't suppose the women are much interested."

"That is not necessarily the case," said Isabella, attempting to save their family. "I have great regard for the Marquess of Wellington. He has a wonderful defensive strategy that has won many battles."

Silence greeted her, and Isabella looked to find her companions — particularly Lydia Fitzgerald and her mother – staring at her with surprise. Warmth suffused her cheeks. "I — I mean to say—"

"You are quite correct," the duke said to her, the surprise on his face turning into a warm smile that she held close to her heart. "I agree with you, Miss Marriott."

She shyly returned his smile, her heart beating fast, but she didn't miss the look the Fitzgerald women sent her way.

"I heard the marquess has quite a propensity for women besides his wife," Lydia Fitzgerald said with her nose in the air before her mother shushed her. It broke the tension of the group, and Isabella suggested they go into dinner, where the meal thankfully went forward without further talk of French-English relations.

Isabella, did, however, find herself seated next to Charles Belrose. He continued to bestow upon her a wide grin, though not much else. He had been invited by her brother, of course, and while he attempted to engage Isabella in conversation throughout the first course, their discussions came to a somewhat grinding halt. The man was too overeager to find much to speak about, and Isabella was growing weary of his ongoing attempts at her affections. The man was kind, but vapid, and she was not in the least bit interested in considering him as a potential husband, no matter what her stepbrother wanted.

Instead, she found her gaze continuing to return to the duke. He was fairly quiet through the dinner, and instead seemed to be listening intently to the conversations around him. He had seated himself near Gerard, which was quite unusual, but Isabella told herself not to read much into it. She just prayed that her stepbrother wouldn't say anything to further embarrass her.

\* \* \*

Despite what she told herself, Isabella went to bed that night with a song in her heart and dreams of a tall, stoic, dark-haired man dancing in her head. She saw him not with his usual seriousness, but with a smile on his face as he looked down at her. It warmed her heart, and other parts of her that she hadn't noticed in quite the same way before. She woke in a sweat, and yet knowing he was connected to her by just two doorways somehow brought her comfort.

She chastised herself. She must not be thinking of such a man, one she could never have. Instead, she should be searching for the missing diary. Her grandmother had always loved puzzles and games. Isabella had begun to suspect that the diary was not lost, but rather, that her grandmother had hidden it somewhere specific, where only she could find it. Perhaps it was not in storerooms or trunks or hidden spaces in the house. Could it be somewhere in plain sight? The library? Her rooms?

Unable to return to sleep as her mind raced, Isabella rose from her bed, stuffing her feet into soft slippers as she began to search around her own room once again. If her grandmother had wanted her to have it — and she really believed she did — then this would have been the ideal room to hide it in. She had searched it before, but perhaps the room needed greater inspection.

Isabella looked once more underneath the mattress, behind paintings, and in the dresser, feeling for hidden drawers or recessed areas. She checked the floorboards and looked within some of the books that lined the shelf beside the bed. Nothing. She sighed. It seemed in all aspects of her life, she was continually striving for something that was just out of her grasp.

She got back in bed and threw herself down on the mattress, flinging her arms behind her in desperation. Would she ever find a way beyond her current state? She just wished she could determine what her next step forward should be.

\* \* \*

BRADLEY WAS GROWING FRUSTRATED. Frustrated with his progress in determining Roger's murderer. The more he spoke with Durand, Belrose, and Rousseau, the more he determined that Durand seemed the most-likely suspect. Belrose was far removed from his French connections, and besides that, he did not seem to be intelligent enough to be any sort of spy, unless he was a talented actor. Rousseau appeared to have remained in England for some time, and in fact brought information to the British. If he was working for the French, he was playing both sides.

Durand, however, had only recently arrived from France, and from a question to the steward, left Miss Marriott's home for periods of time. From the conversation at dinner the previous night, he had shown some sympathy to the French Emperor, though he was quick to recover. How to prove it, though? Could he find some sort of record of Durand's whereabouts the night Roger was shot?

He was also growing frustrated with his attraction to Isabella Marriott. The woman had no idea of what she was doing to him. Every time she smiled, bit her lip, or walked in front of him, he felt an ache in his loins as he desired her more than the time before. Of course, there was nothing to be done about it. He was not the type of man to have a dalliance with a lady like her and he had no current wish to wed.

He did wish, however, he could simply bed her to get her out of his mind. She was tantalizing him, though quite unknowingly. However, her position being what it was, he resolved to try to keep her at a distance so that he could focus on his true purpose. It seemed the fates were against him, however, as every time he tried to remove himself from her, something drew them closer together.

The next morning dawned bright and warm, and Bradley was looking out his window at the gardens when he saw a shape moving below his window. He leaned out further, shocked to catch a glimpse of Miss Marriott as she made her way around the rose bushes and deeper into the gardens. What was she doing out there at this time of the morning? Most ladies he knew slept much later. Before he could even think of what he was doing, he was dressed and down the stairs, searching for the garden doors. He told himself he was seeking her out for further research into Durand.

When he found the doors, he took his time on the pathway, as if he was making his own random stroll through the garden. When he finally reached her, he made a show of surprise at seeing her.

"Miss Marriott! We must stop running into one another like this," he said, noticing the faint blush on her cheeks.

"Your grace," she said, inclining her head. "I hope you slept well."

"I tried," he said with a sigh, as he looked up at her from beneath slanted brows. "My thoughts were preoccupied, however."

"Oh," she said, her cheeks turning even rosier, which was quite becoming on her. "I- I'm sorry to hear that."

"Miss Marriott… you intrigue me."

"I do?" her eyes flew up to his in shock he didn't understand.

"You do. You are enchanting," he said, the words out of his mouth before he even knew what he was saying as he drew closer to her. "I should like to know more about you."

"There is not much to tell, your grace," she said, looking down at the flowers in the garden bed below her.

"I wish you would call me something other than 'your grace,'" he said. "Perhaps Bradley?"

"Oh, but I could never," she replied with a quick shake of her head. "It would not be right."

"Carrington, then?"

"I will try," she said with a nod, though the color that was so becoming on her remained in her cheeks.

"How long has it been since you lived here as a child?"

"About six years. My mother passed when I was young, and my father — my father chose to leave for France for business purposes. When I returned two years ago following his death, I took over the house once more. Thankfully the steward had remained, and we had a very small staff looking after its upkeep. It took some work to refurbish it to living conditions once more, but I have so enjoyed it."

"Until your stepbrother returned?"

"I suppose to some degree, yes. Although I do still have my enjoyments. Like this garden for instance," she said, as she swept her hand out overtop the beds of colorful flowers and hedges in front of them.

"Do you not have a gardener?"

"I do, of course. But I enjoy working with him, planning and planting and even weeding when I have the opportunity. I love seeing things grow from nothing. When I returned here, these gardens were completely overrun, and it has been quite satisfying to see them return to their former glory."

He saw the pride in her face, and understood the rewards of hard work. He spent more time overseeing his estates than most noblemen did — at least, he had, before he had been called to work with the Foreign Office. He had been proud of what he was doing for his country as well, before his efforts had led to tragedy.

"I must ask, Miss Marriott," he said, with as much nonchalance as he could muster, "what is your brother's interest in England? Forgive me for asking, but most Frenchmen who come to England do so because they strongly oppose France's position. Your brother, however, seems to admire Little Boney."

Her face clouded and closed off to him. "He is not my brother but my stepbrother," she repeated again. "I have truly only known him for a few years now. He claims he stays to find a wife and to look after me, although I am far from requiring a chaperone, let alone having someone like him nearby. I have an inkling that he has his eyes on my inheritance, although how he plans to benefit from it, I do not know."

Bradley nodded, trying to focus on her words, though he was having a hard time concentrating. They had stopped walking and now were far in the recesses of the garden, hidden from the house by the hedges and trees between them. She was close to him now, her head bent over the plants below her. Whether she was studying them or hiding her face, he wasn't sure.

He reached down and grasped her chin with his finger and thumb. He tilted her face up toward his, and he saw her eyes widen in astonishment. He bent his head down to her, eager to place a kiss on those lips that tempted him so. She half closed her eyes as she leaned in toward him, accepting the unspoken invitation. He leaned down and —

"Isabella! Isabella?"

The voice cut through the air, breaking the spell that had caught hold of both of them. Isabella took a step back, as she turned her head frantically for the source of the voice.

"It's Olivia," she said, somewhat apologetically. "We were to meet in the gardens this morning and I'm afraid I had quite forgotten. Thank you for the walk, your grace, ah — Carrington. Good day."

And with that, she turned and ran as if being chased. Bradley smiled until he realized his infatuation with her had, once again, completely taken him off course. He sighed and ran a hand over his face. This would never do.

# CHAPTER 8

Isabella was quite pleased that the following afternoon an outing was planned for both the men and women, allowing them all the opportunity for a respite from the house. She loved the outdoors, but it was difficult to find time away when she was expected to entertain the women who were staying with them – many more than she would have ever predicted.

Despite the fact the house party was being held by Isabella and Gerard, who were not particularly high in society, the guests were intrigued by the fact the mysteriously aloof Duke of Carrington was attending. It was rare he frequented gatherings such as this, and so drew the crowd.

They planned to ride through the woodland close to Isabella's home that afternoon, a bit of a tour for those who had never seen the property before. While it was small, Isabella was proud of it, though Gerard was quick to play the host.

The party gathered at the stables — all who were joining that afternoon, with the exception of Olivia. Knowing her friend and her propensity for lateness, Isabella urged the rest of them to continue on as she waited for her. Minutes later, Olivia arrived, holding onto her bonnet as she flew from the house.

"My goodness, Isabella, I am truly sorry! My maid could not find my riding habit until much too late, and by the time she had it ready it was—"

"Don't fret," Isabella responded, placing a hand on her arm to calm her. "We shall catch up to the rest of them. And, it should give us time away from the others to truly speak our thoughts."

She smiled warmly as they mounted their horses and continued on the trail at a trot to catch the others, who would be moving at a much slower pace.

"Isabella," Olivia began, "no more putting me off. You *must* tell me what is happening between you and the Duke of Carrington. Did this begin the night of the ball? Had you met him previously and kept it hidden? Did he come to this party for you?"

"Stop!" Isabella said, laughing as she attempted to stem Olivia's flow of words. "There is nothing between me and the duke, nor will there ever be."

"Oh?" Olivia raised one eyebrow. "That is not what I would have gathered from what I came upon in the garden. My apologies for that, by the way."

"You came upon nothing," said Isabella, growing serious. "The duke is... a gentleman, and yes, of course I find him incredibly handsome, as any woman would. He is intelligent and respectful and while serious, he has such quick wit. But he is not for me, Olivia. If he does not know already, he will soon learn of my father's failed business schemes and his removal to France. I have told him some of it myself, though was too ashamed to explain the full story."

"How do you know he does not already know of this?"

"Would he be speaking to me if he did?"

"I believe he would. If he is the man you think him to be, then he would not care about your father."

"He is a *duke*, Olivia. He should not be interested in any viscount's daughter, particularly one whose family has found such shame."

Olivia sighed and shook her head. "Does he bring you joy?"

"Yes," Isabella couldn't lie. "There is something about him that makes me feel at peace, even when Gerard is about."

"Then you must keep yourself open to what may come. I believe he likely cares for you. He seems to prefer your company over others in the group. Why, last night at dinner he could barely take his eyes off you! Lady Fitzgerald and her daughter seem to be quite put out."

They were coming upon the group in front of them now, and Isabella shushed Olivia. She couldn't miss the duke's tall frame, riding his horse with ease. He was riding beside Lydia, of course, and Isabella gave Olivia a pointed look. The two of them looked well together, her fair hair and his dark countenance. Their match would make sense, and Isabella suddenly felt like a fool for thinking that the duke would have any interest in her.

She heard Olivia murmur beside her and she turned to face her. "What is it?"

"Lord Kenley," she said with a grin, as Isabella noted her eyes were fixed on the man in question, riding at the edge of the group. "I quite enjoy watching his backside from here."

"Olivia!" Isabella scolded, but couldn't keep from laughing. Olivia was quite forward, and her poor mother didn't know what to do with her, as most young men were put off by her outspoken ways.

The smile left her face as she saw Gerard look back at

them from the front of the group, and he circled around to speak with them.

"Lady Olivia," he said, nodding at Olivia dismissively. The two of them despised one another, and neither kept their dislike hidden. "Isabella," he addressed her. "Where have you been? I have no idea where I'm going through these overgrown woods."

"You wanted to lead the party," she replied with exasperation. "I was simply waiting for one of our guests."

He gave Olivia a look as if to say that she was not considered much of a guest and that she had inconvenienced the rest of them.

"Well, take over now," he said as a command. "Or at the very least tell me where to go and what to say to these people."

Isabella bit her lip to keep back a retort, but not before she noted that the duke had overheard the exchange as he was riding back toward them.

"Durand," he said in a stern tone. "Is all well?"

"Of course," he said, all smiles now as he turned to the duke. "I was simply concerned about what had been keeping my sister."

Olivia rolled her eyes behind his back and Isabella tried to suppress a smile.

"I have no issue with taking the lead," Isabella said to diffuse the tension between them all. "Please, follow me."

She rode to the front of the group and began to explain all that her land had to offer.

\* \* \*

BRADLEY DRESSED for dinner that night with a multitude of thoughts and emotions running through him. He was pleased that he seemed to be growing closer to Miss Marriott, and had managed to extract some information from her on her stepbrother. He was annoyed with himself, however, at his guilt, for he could not keep himself from seeing her as more than a source. The more he thought of her, the less he was focused on determining whether Durand was involved in Roger's death.

After learning more about the man, he realized he *wanted* him to be involved, to be the one he was searching for. Durand was the type of man Bradley had never liked. He was a disrespectful bully and was clearly using his stepsister and taking advantage of her situation. He didn't know how Gerard planned to access Isabella's fortune if it was tied to her marriage, but clearly something was afoot. Perhaps he had some agreement with a man like Belrose? But if that was the case, why did he seem fine with the fact that he and Isabella were growing closer? It seemed almost as if he had given up on Belrose and was pushing her toward him. It didn't make any sense. What did Gerard expect from him?

Lord Fitzgerald had told him more about Isabella's family during the tour of the grounds, before she had joined the riding party. Bradley had previously believed that there was something dishonorable regarding the viscount's departure to France, but he wasn't sure what it was. Failed businesses were unfortunate, to be sure, but this secret was not nearly as scandalous as what he had assumed it to be. When he questioned Isabella's inheritance, Fitzgerald had begrudgingly told him that the viscount had found success in France, rebuilding his fortunes there. It had, however, done nothing for his reputation in England.

It wasn't difficult to realize that Fitzgerald assumed that sharing information about the viscount would keep Bradley from Isabella. It didn't seem to be a secret that he had some intention toward her, and Bradley couldn't even lie to himself any longer about how much he wanted her. He had, in fact, stopped thinking of her as Miss Marriott, but instead as Isabella. He would have to ensure that he never said such a thing aloud.

He knew she had left France and returned to England before her stepbrother. Had it been a planned escape from him, or was there a chance she had returned to do reconnaissance for the French? He wanted to believe that could never be the case, but she had spent some years there and would have reason to be thankful to the country due to its acceptance of her father. He hoped he could convince her to trust him enough to share her plans and reasoning with him.

He knocked on the door of Alastair's room before dinner, in order to have a moment to speak with him alone. His friend seemed to be quite enjoying himself. Bradley filled him in on all that he had found out, leaving out additional details of his moments alone with Isabella.

Alastair's bedchamber was warm and welcoming, but not as grand as the duke's. The furnishings, while well kept, were beginning to show their age. Bradley's respect for Miss Marriott grew as he reflected on the effort she had put into maintaining her home despite her financial constraints.

"What do you think?" he asked his friend, eager for an unbiased opinion on the woman in question.

"Do I think she could be working for the French?" Alastair asked, as he seated himself in a straight-back mahogany chair across from Bradley, crossing one leg over the other. "It's possible. However, from what I can tell, she and her stepbrother do not get along well, and I would wager it more likely he is the one we are looking for, and he uses her as a front."

Bradley nodded his head in agreement. "Perhaps you could find out more about Miss Marriott, from someone other than herself."

"And how might I do that?"

"Get closer with her friend, Lady Olivia. From what I gather, they have known one another for many years. Perhaps she will provide you with more information."

"Ah, Lady Olivia," said Alastair with a wolfish grin, "that, I can do. The woman is a beauty, and a fiery one at that."

"Perhaps don't get *too* close," Bradley said with a frown in warning. "Her father is an earl himself. I doubt he would appreciate you simply playing with his daughter."

Alastair raised both hands in the air.

"Understood," he said. "I may be considered a rake, but I am no fool. Come, Carrington, let us go find our ladies."

Bradley rolled his eyes, questioning his decision to ask for Alastair's help, and followed his friend out of the room.

He noted that evening that Alastair took particular notice of Lady Olivia, who seemed to be quite pleased with his attentions. They flirted through the meal, and she gave him a little wave after dinner as the ladies retired to the drawing room and the men to the library.

"Did you find out anything of note?" he asked Alastair, as they hung back from the rest of the gentlemen.

"I have found that I thoroughly enjoy the company of Lady Olivia," said Alastair with a smug look on his face, before taking in his friend's stern expression. "Fine, fine, Carrington. I did nothing that would reflect poorly on me. I can tell you that Lady Olivia quite despises Durand, and noted that Miss Marriott spends her life trying to avoid her stepbrother. She mentioned that Miss Marriott has no intention to ever return to France, as she has many painful memories there of her stepbrother, as well as the death of her father and stepmother, who was actually not that bad of a woman. Oh, and I did manage to discover that Miss Marriott has not left the area in some time, though her stepbrother is quite well known as a traveler, and the household servants are instructed to hide any ledgers or household information from the man. Is that helpful?"

"Very much so," said Bradley with a nod, as he stretched a hand out toward the library. "Now, come, let us see what more we can extract from these men."

## CHAPTER 9

Isabella bit her lip as she lifted another stack of dusty books from the corner of the room, just managing to stifle a sneeze. It was early morning and she had already been awake for some hours, searching for her grandmother's diary. It had proved difficult to find time to search, what with the house party going on, and Isabella had been forced to wait until the early hours of the morning to continue looking for it.

Of course, that meant rising with dawn which, after a late evening entertaining their guests, made her extremely tired, but the need to find the diary was pressing. She wanted to escape Gerard and, if she could only find this box and the heirlooms within, then she could make her escape and start again.

Flicking through the heavy tomes, just in case the diary was there, Isabella let her mind wander to what life could be like in the Americas. She had heard a few things about it, and it sounded like quite a wonderful place, with many opportunities for women, although it would require hard work on her part. The hardest part would be leaving behind her home and all of the memories it held, but she would build a new one.

It would be a place where she could start over, never having to worry about marrying and releasing the rest of her fortune. Finding the box would mean that she could live as an independent woman. She might even take on a new name so that Gerard would never be able to trace her. Finally, she would be entirely free from him.

For a moment, a picture of the duke fell into her mind and Isabella could not help but wonder whether he might be someone with whom she could share her concerns.

The day they had both walked into the same dressing room had been embarrassing, to say the least, but she had found words tumbling from her mouth without being able to stop them, saying more about her stepbrother than she'd intended. There was something about the man that brought her vulnerability to the fore. He appeared trustworthy and honest, not throwing back glass after glass of liquor as her brother did nor tossing his money around during games of cards.

And the almost-kiss in the garden. Isabella sighed. What might have happened had Olivia not come upon them, she wasn't sure, but she was now longing to have the opportunity to come that close to the duke once more.

Shaking her head to herself, Isabella lifted up a dusty old trunk and tried not to scream at the sight of three coin-sized spiders that immediately crawled for cover. She had become well used to the creatures during her searches, but still was not particularly enamored by the sight of them. Suppressing a shudder, she waited until the spiders had crawled out of sight before reaching into the trunk to lift out yet more books.

This was one of the many rooms she had yet to search, but it proved to be hopeless. She spent another hour looking into old trunks and drawers but found only old clothes and books so torn and illegible they belonged in the fire. There were even old accounts from when her father had run into difficulties, which she chose to put back into the deepest, darkest recesses of the dusty old trunks. She did not want to be reminded of that time.

The sun was bright now, and Isabella knew it would soon be time to return to her room. It was still early enough for Gerard to be asleep in his chamber, but she did not want to take any chances by lingering for longer than she should. Brushing at her skirts, she bit back a laugh at the dust cloud that rose from them. It was just as well the servants knew not to clean this particular dress on a daily basis, given that she wore it each time she had to search another room. It had marks all over it and probably held more dust than the cloths the maids used to clean.

Perhaps she would ask her maid to give it a thorough beating before she put it on again so that the dust would not cling to her skin as it did this very moment. She was going to have to bathe, which meant cold water in a bowl and a cloth instead of gently steaming water in the large tub. That was something of a luxury according to Gerard and, on top of which, not something that she was willing to ask of her staff, not when they already had so much to do.

Shutting the door quietly, Isabella began to make her way back to her room, barely making a sound as she walked. The house was still and silent, so the last thing she expected was to see the Duke of Carrington step out from the library, closing the door with great care. She paused in her steps, waiting until he saw her before giving him a tense smile of greeting.

"Ah, Miss Marriott," he murmured softly, his eyes traveling the length of her dirty gown, "good morning."

Isabella frowned, wondering what on earth he was doing leaving the library at this time of the day.

"Good morning, your grace," she said, suddenly very aware, as he turned to face her, that he was only in an open-necked shirt and pantaloons. Heat mounted in her face as she looked away, knowing that she should simply walk past him and return to her room. Being alone like this was not a good idea and yet she couldn't tear herself away.

"Have you been... cleaning?" he asked, lifting one eyebrow.

"Oh!" she exclaimed, covering her mouth with her hand as the sound bounced off the walls. "No, indeed, your grace. I was...." Her mouth grew dry as she realized she was going to have to think of some kind of explanation for her appearance, glancing down at her dusty and dirty gown. "I was looking for something," she finished, lamely.

He nodded, his eyebrows meeting as he frowned. "I see," he said, slowly. "And did you find it?"

"N-no, unfortunately, I didn't," she stammered, hating that she was being so foolish. "I thank you for your concern, your grace. I should go and change."

"Of course," he smiled at her, and Isabella felt her legs go weak with a mixture of relief and delight, "and it's Carrington, remember?"

"Carrington, yes," she repeated.

It did not seem that he was about to start questioning her further on what she had been doing, although she could not help but be curious as to his own actions. Was he some kind of avid reader?

"I could not sleep," he explained, as though reading her mind. "The library was nearby and I thought perhaps a good book might help me pass the next few hours."

Isabella's gaze drifted to his hands, seeing no evidence of a book. "You did not find what you were looking for either, then? Nothing to your liking in my father's rows of bookshelves, then, your gr— Carrington?"

She looked up at him again, surprised to see him glance away from her, looking a little awkward all of a sudden. He placed his hands behind his back and cleared his throat, looking for all the world like a little boy who had been caught taking something he should not.

"No," he said, with a slight shrug. "I'm afraid I did not. I found myself growing weary again and so decided to return to my room."

"I see," she murmured, not entirely convinced that he was telling her the truth. There was something a little odd about the scenario they currently found themselves in, and Isabella got the feeling that neither of them particularly wanted to share the true reason for being out in the hallway at such an unorthodox hour. Normally at ease around one another, the air this morning was filled with an awkward tension. They looked at each other for a moment before he cleared his throat once more and stepped aside, holding his arm out so that she might pass by him.

"Thank you," Isabella said, softly, daring a look at him as she walked past.

To her surprise, at the last moment he caught her arm, halting her in her steps. She did not know what to say or what to do, trapped by the intensity of his gaze, her heart fluttering in her chest. His breath caressed her cheek as she looked up at him, too aware of his open shirt and bare skin. She stood still, aware of how his fingers released their tight grip on her arm and slowly began to caress her as he drew her closer to him.

She did not know what she was doing, but found her hand reaching up to brush lightly against the bare skin at his collar. She had never touched a man before, not in such an intimate fashion, and the brief dance of her fingers against the hard plains of his chest had her gasping in surprise. Heat rushed through her, sparking from where her skin touched his.

She heard his breath catch, as though he too felt the same as she and, feeling a little bolder, Isabella ran her fingers under the open collar, her heart quickening in her chest. A strange, unbidden desire to remove his shirt entirely began to wash over her, and, when it became too great, Isabella dropped her hand and tried to step back, only for him to tighten his grip on her other hand. Unable to convince herself to escape from him, and unable to dampen the raging inferno that was sweeping over her, Isabella was forced to look into his eyes, seeing a deep passion settling there. It was a look of intensity that took her breath away.

"Miss Marriott," he said, so quietly that she had to strain to hear him as his eyes drifted to her mouth. "I –" he looked as though he was about to say something more, that he was about to explain something, but instead, he simply leaned down, pulling her into him as his lips descended on hers.

Isabella's eyes closed of their own accord, as she swayed a little unsteadily at the searing heat of his mouth. In truth, it was the culmination of a kiss that had begun the moment their eyes locked at the Fitzgeralds' ball. It was hard, but quick, gone in a moment though enough to overwhelm her. Her eyes remained closed as she savored the moment, her first experience of being kissed devastating her senses. Her body grew still, her heart beating so loudly she was sure the sound echoed around the hallway.

He raised his head briefly, and Isabella blinked up at him, wondering if he was going to speak. As his eyes raked over her face, there was confusion in his expression, as though he had been as surprised as she at his actions. But before she could speak to him of it, his mouth captured hers once more.

There was a fierceness in his kiss that almost brought her

to her knees. She gave the wall behind her all of her weight as he angled his head, his tongue brushing the seam of her mouth. Isabella gasped in shock, her eyes flying open, and when she let him in, his tongue caressed hers in an intimate love play. She felt something stir in her center, and she pressed into him, yearning for more.

His hips ground into hers, and she felt the result of his desire for her. He leaned into her now, his hands on the wall as he trapped her against his body. She felt secure in the frame of his arms, and she reached out to pull him tighter to her – only for the contact to break and quick footsteps begin to echo around the hallway. He was gone.

Isabella opened her eyes slowly, only to see the duke retreat around the corner, without even a backward glance. Blinking, Isabella touched her lower lip carefully, still stunned at what they had done. Why had he left so abruptly? To her, it had been more... *everything* than she had ever experienced in her life, leaving her with a mix of confused emotions. Perhaps, however, he was a man well used to pressing such affections on a lady, and they meant very little to him – but his hasty withdrawal still surprised her.

Wandering back to her room, Isabella smiled to herself despite her confusion over his abrupt departure.

"I just hope he was not trying to distract me from what he was doing in the library at this hour," she said aloud, closing the door of her bedchamber behind her. It felt quite wrong to have such doubts after he had kissed her, but there was something about the duke that would not stop niggling at her mind.

He was an enigma, confusing and mysterious – and, after this particular meeting, Isabella felt sure that there was more to him than met the eye.

And he had been the one to cause it.

# CHAPTER 10

"*A*h, my lord duke!"

Bradley stiffened as Gerard Durand greeted him, despising this man even more every time he interacted with him. Durand was over-the-top cordial to him, but he was aware it was a façade after hearing the way he spoke to Isabella and the servants.

"Good afternoon, Durand," he said, not smiling in return. "I hope you had a pleasant morning."

"Indeed, indeed," Durand replied, slapping Bradley on the shoulder as though they were old friends. "And how are you finding my house party, your grace? I hope it is to your satisfaction!"

Bradley could not help that his thoughts immediately turned to Isabella, with a stirring in his loins that he forced himself to ignore. He should not have left her as he had, but it was the only way to stop himself from taking things any further.

He cleared his throat. "It is very enjoyable. I thank you for the invitation."

Durand nodded but kept his eyes on Bradley. "You have been some time away from England, I hear."

"Not too long," Bradley replied, a slight warning ringing in his ears. "I went to visit a friend."

"And where does your friend live?"

Wondering whether Durand was asking questions to be polite, or for another, more nefarious reason, Bradley chose to be as discreet as possible. "Some distance away, I must confess. I am glad to be home." He forced a smile on his face, seeing the way that Durand's eyes glinted with a sudden steely look.

"Well, I do hope that your return has been an enjoyable one," Durand continued, sounding quite sincere. "Have you a lot of business to attend to, or does your steward look after that?"

"My stewards are very thorough, indeed," Bradley answered, with the air of one who was quite at ease. "It means I am able to come and go as I please, although I do enjoy staying on top of all that goes on."

"I see," Durand murmured, thoughtfully. "I am glad, then, that you could spare the time to join us."

"Not in the least," Bradley replied, putting on an icy smile. "I could think of nothing better but to spend a few days in such…" his eyes roved around the room, picking out Lord Belrose and Lord Rousseau, "*interesting* company." Bradley let his gaze settle on Durand once more. "And you, Durand, have you had the opportunity to return to your home country as of late?"

Durand was now frowning, studying Bradley as though he could not quite make him out. Pleased, Bradley's smile widened just as they were joined by Lord Kenley, however Durand took the opportunity to avoid Bradley's question and Bradley cursed his friend's timing.

"Good afternoon, Durand," Alastair said, smiling. "What

plans have you for the rest of the day? It is a very fine day, to say the least!"

"It is indeed," Durand replied, drawing in a breath and settling his shoulders again. "In fact, some of the gentlemen were thinking of going out for a ride." His brows rose in question as he turned to face Bradley once again. "Would you care to join us?"

Bradley, thinking that this would be an excellent opportunity to continue his search of the house, appeared to consider it for a moment, before shaking his head. "Alas, I think not. I am a little tired this afternoon and would value the opportunity to spend a few hours resting before this evening's entertainment."

The dismay on the man's face was more than obvious, although he shrugged as though he did not mind. "But of course," he replied, quickly, "my library is at your disposal."

"I thank you," Bradley murmured, delighted that he might have the opportunity to search a little more. The ladies would be occupied with their own conversation, which meant that he would not have to worry about another temptation with Miss Marriott.

"And what of you, Lord Kenley?" Durand asked, looking at Alastair. "Might you join us?"

There was a brief hesitation. Bradley, catching Alastair's eye, gave him the smallest of nods and, at once, Alastair agreed to go riding with the other gentlemen.

"Wonderful!" Durand exclaimed, sounding quite delighted. "Shall we say in an hour, then?"

"Of course," Alastair replied. "I look forward to it." Waiting until Durand had walked away to greet his other guests, Alastair turned to Bradley with a look of concern on his face, motioning for him to walk across the room, where they found a quieter place behind a large potted plant. "He seemed very keen for you to join us on the ride, Carrington."

Bradley could not help but agree, his gaze still on Durand. "Mayhap he is just being friendly," he said, even though his intuition told him that he was quite wrong even to suggest such a thing. "And I have noticed that he watches both myself and Miss Marriott very closely. Perhaps he just wishes me to wed her and is attempting to ingratiate himself to sweeten my affections toward her."

Alastair turned to face him, surprise on his face. "Affections? You mean, you truly care for Miss Marriott?"

Realizing that he had slipped up, Bradley shook his head. "No," he said, firmly. "I do not hold any affections for Miss Marriott."

Unfortunately for him, Alastair did not look convinced. "Are you quite sure?" he said, in a voice that betrayed his disbelief. "You are very often in her company and –"

"That is just so that I can get close to her stepbrother," Bradley interrupted, a swipe of his hand dismissing Alastair's words. "However, she is good company and I find her conversation very interesting, but there is nothing more to it than that. And, it seems to be working. She has imparted a great deal of information that I have found very useful."

Shaking his head, Alastair sighed heavily. "Be that as it may, I do wish you'd be honest with yourself, Carrington. I am not quite sure that even *you* believe what you're saying about the lady. I have never seen you act in such a way before, I am quite sure."

Bradley grunted, putting his back against the wall and sighing. He was not going to convince Alastair, it seemed, but that did not particularly matter.

He heard a brush of skirts to their left, but turning to look around the plant beside him, he saw no one. He shrugged his shoulders, but couldn't help the feeling of unease that washed over him.

"You don't suppose anyone can hear our conversation, do

you?" he said, cursing his foolishness at speaking so openly amongst the group of people.

To his very great surprise, Alastair chuckled. "I don't believe so. But you see," he laughed, "I knew you were not as unattached as you said! You would not feel this guilty about what someone may have heard if you did not feel *something* for her."

Bradley opened his mouth to refute the idea, but Alastair only laughed, slapped him on the back, and walked away, leaving him alone.

\* \* \*

IT WAS NOT until much later that Bradley found himself in the library, sitting alone with a book in his lap and a brandy by his elbow. The gentlemen had taken more than an hour to leave for the stables, and he had then waited another half hour to ensure the house was quiet. The ladies, from what he knew, were all ensconced in the drawing room. He had not taken great pains to get to know any of them particularly well and, given that his focus was entirely elsewhere, could not even recall everyone's name.

He did realize the Fitzgeralds were particularly intent on drawing him closer to Lady Lydia, but he had done his best to remain aloof and uninterested. She was a girl, while he was instead much more focused on a *woman*. Well, focused on trying to resist a woman.

While he was still holding himself back from the feelings he had for her, he could certainly admit that he desired Isabella with all of his being. His resolve to stay away from her was weakening but he was determined.

He put his book down and rose, his eyes roving over the great number of shelves. He had already searched one half of the library in the early hours of the morning, only retreating to his room when he knew the maids would soon be up and about. However, the urge to check Durand's study was too strong to ignore. It was the perfect opportunity, given that the man was out riding.

Usually, Bradley would have had Alastair with him to ensure that he was alerted to anyone nearby but this might be the best he could do. It would have looked a little odd if they both refused to ride, for, if Durand was the man Bradley was searching for, it could alert him to the true reason for their presence at the house party.

The clicking of his shoes on the polished marble floor made him cringe, even though he was now quite alone. There did not seem to be many servants around and Bradley was grateful that he had learned the layout of the house prior to this. Making his way to the study, he turned to glance over his shoulder, an uncomfortable prickling sensation racing down his spine.

There was no one present, however, and, with a hand that was a little slick with sweat, Bradley tried the door handle. To his very great surprise, it opened at once. He would have thought that Durand would have locked his study in order to keep everything secure, but apparently he was not as secretive — or as careful — as Bradley had expected.

Stepping inside, Bradley drew in a sharp breath, expecting someone to be within, but the room was completely empty. Closing the door quietly, he surveyed the contents of the study, wondering where to start.

It was quite a comfortable room, not at all as Bradley had expected from a man like Durand. Although, Isabella had said it was originally her father's study. Perhaps Durand had not changed much. There were portraits of men Bradley expected were ancestors on the walls, a desk and comfortable plush wingback chairs the only pieces of furniture.

Moving to Durand's desk, he sat down in his chair and began to pull open the various drawers.

It seemed they were empty of anything of note.

There was nothing much to be found – accounts, letters and the like, including a few personal letters that brought a chuckle to Bradley's lips and warmth to his face. Durand was involved in some lewd sexual acts, that was certain, but that did not make him a murderer. Bradley probably shouldn't be reading such things but it was necessary to discover the truth about Durand. Was he, truthfully, loyal to the Crown? Or was his connection to France still strong?

Getting to his feet and ensuring that all the drawers were tightly closed, Bradley wandered to the left of the room, seeing a heavy drape that looked as though it was covering a large window, except that it seemed to be a curious position. Frowning, Bradley walked toward it and, with a tug, saw that the curtain, in fact, hid what appeared to be a very large cabinet.

His heart slammed into his chest as a buzz of excitement flooded his veins. Had Durand something to hide? And, if so, was Bradley to find the evidence he'd been searching for here? Taking hold of the cabinet handle, he tugged it open, surprised at the amount of strength he needed to simply open the door. His gaze flickered over the contents, seeing a large empty space at the bottom of the cabinet, but three heavy looking drawers were above it. The drawers, however, were locked. Frowning, Bradley inspected them a little more closely, seeing that they each had a tiny and intricate-looking lock. There was no way he would be able to access the contents unless he was somehow able to open the drawers. He did not want Durand to see that he had broken in which meant that, somehow, he was going to have to find a key.

A sudden sound of voices had him frozen in place as his pulse pounded. Was that not Durand's voice? What was he doing back at the house so early? Frantic, Bradley looked at the door, seeing the handle begin to turn slowly.

"I don't know what you are complaining about, Isabella!" came Durand's harsh tones. "The man is clearly besotted with you and you are doing nothing to encourage him, which is quite unacceptable. For goodness sake, girl, don't you want to marry?"

Unable to make out Isabella's reply, Bradley knew he needed to hide — and fast — and pushed the heavy drape back into its proper place. For a moment, he thought about hiding within the cabinet, but what if Durand had to fetch something from it? He would be found out at once.

However, the handle turned, Durand's voice became clearer, and Bradley had no other choice but to quickly seat himself in the bottom of the cabinet and pull the door closed behind him. Darkness hid him and Bradley could only pray that Durand would not come to the cabinet and find him hiding there.

# CHAPTER 11

Bradley hardly dared to breathe, to prevent making any noise. If Durand found him, the game was up. How he was meant to escape from this situation without Durand noticing him he simply did not know, as he desperately hoped that Durand would leave the study soon.

"That wretched girl," he heard Durand mutter, evidently talking about Isabella. "The sooner she gives in, the sooner I shall have her wealth."

Frowning to himself, Bradley wondered what it was Durand was talking about. Isabella had never mentioned a fortune before now, although he knew that she was the owner of the estate and her father had left her something of an inheritance, but it was dependent upon her marriage. And how did Durand intend to get his hands on her wealth?

Before he could consider the matter further, another voice met his ears — one he recognized. Charles Belrose.

"You wanted to see me?"

"Yes. Thank you for leaving the other gentlemen. I know how much you wanted to ride."

Charles murmured something that Bradley did not quite

catch, although the whining tone of his voice let Bradley know that the man felt quite inferior to Durand.

"Now, have you made any progress regarding my stepsister?"

"She talks to me, but no more so than any other gentleman," Belrose replied. "Though I have never mentioned my intentions."

"Then you need to step things up," came Durand's firm reply. "Come now, Belrose! What I am asking of you is not exactly difficult."

There was a loud and heavy sigh. "Your sister – "

"*Step*sister," Durand interrupted, gruffly.

"Very well. Your stepsister does not seem particularly interested in me, especially when the Duke of Carrington has been paying her so much attention."

A snort met Bradley's ears, as he listened intently, the hair on the back of his neck beginning to stand up at the mention of his name.

"The duke will not be in the picture for long, Belrose," Durand said, calmly. "Her affections for him will actually work well with our plans. She will need someone to turn to soon, and you are to be that man. I am quite sure you will be wed before the summer."

There was a prolonged silence. Bradley could almost imagine the way that Charles Belrose was staring at Gerard Durand, although he could not tell whether Belrose was surprised at what Durand had said. Was something to happen to him to cause Isabella such tragedy?

"You know I do not want to be a part of your schemes, Durand," Belrose said, after some minutes. "Whatever they are, I am loyal to the Crown."

"And yet, you have French blood running through your veins," Durand replied, witheringly. "You may say you are loyal, Belrose, but I know better. I know that you will bend in whatever way I tell you, simply so that you might call my sister your wife."

"That is not true," Charles said, weakly.

A loud, obnoxious laugh came from Durand. "Oh, but it is," he replied after his laughter had died away. "You know what I can do to you, Belrose." There was a pause, and Bradley felt a spurt of anger push through his veins. Durand was a villain, there was no doubt about it.

"However, I will keep my plans to myself," Durand continued, as though he were offering Belrose some kind of marvelous gift. "Your constitution could not take it, I think. You have always been a weak man, Belrose, which is precisely why I chose you for my stepsister."

Bradley waited for Belrose to respond, to defend himself, but instead there only came the sound of footsteps and the opening and closing of the door. A cold sweat broke out over his skin, as Bradley realized just how weak Belrose truly was. Whatever it was Durand had planned, he had chosen Belrose particularly because he would not fight Durand's intentions. Did that mean that Belrose might, in fact, be willing to talk to Bradley about Durand if Bradley pressed him hard enough?

"What is it now?" he heard Durand exclaim, the sound of a chair scraping across the floor as he got to his feet. He heard the butler mutter something, only for Durand to curse in frustration and leave the room, the door slamming closed.

Bradley was frozen for a moment, unable to move, worried that Durand might suddenly return to the study without warning. Should he try and escape now, in the hope that Durand would not return?

Carefully pushing open the cabinet door, he pulled himself out with a groan, his muscles complaining about the cramped position they had held. Closing the cabinet door, he pulled back the curtain just a little, seeing the study door closed. With no sound coming from the hallway, he crept toward the door, not knowing what he would say if Durand came back in unexpectedly.

Pressing his ear to the heavy wooden door, he held his breath and listened. Hearing nothing, Bradley drew in a sharp breath and opened the door, stepping outside and closing it behind him in one smooth motion. To his very great relief, there was not a soul present in the hallway, and Bradley sagged a little against the door.

"Your grace?"

He jumped and turned sharply, seeing Miss Marriott exit from a room to his right, a look of surprise on her face upon seeing him standing at the door to her brother's study. Realizing that his hand was still on the door handle, he gingerly released it and gave her a small smile.

"Ah, Miss Marriott. We meet again." He tried to keep his tone nonchalant, even though he could see the surprise and confusion etched on her face. "Are you having a pleasant afternoon?"

There was no answering smile on her face, no blush to her cheeks. Instead, she looked straight at him, her mouth in a tight line.

"Were you in the study?"

"What?" he asked, feigning ignorance. "Oh, yes, I was. I mean, I was looking for your stepbrother, that was all."

She frowned at once. "He is out riding, as I believe you know."

"Are you quite sure?" he replied, trying to sound surprised. "I was certain I heard him a moment ago and came out of the library in search of him."

The frown did not leave her face, and, to his consternation, she narrowed her eyes in suspicion. "I don't think –" she began, only for Durand's voice to echo down the hallway to them both, stunning her into silence.

Bradley smiled, ignoring the way his heart slammed into his chest. If she told her brother that he had been in his study, it could prove fatal to his investigation.

"However, that can wait," he said, abruptly, catching her hand and placing it on his arm. "I had hoped to catch you alone, Miss Marriott, so that we might talk about this morning's events." He would not normally discuss a kiss with a woman, of course, but it was the only thing that came to mind that would distract her from his whereabouts. "I do hope I did not upset you," he continued, softly, steering her back toward the library and hoping they would be able to enter it before Durand arrived.

"Oh, well," she began, sounding flustered. "I was a little taken aback, I will confess. I am not used to such... attentions."

Bradley looked down at her but her face was turned away from him. However, what he could see of her cheek was turning a light shade of dusky pink, convincing him that she was not at all unaffected by what he had done.

Managing to close the library door behind him, he let go of her arm and cleared his throat. The truth was, he was not quite sure why he had kissed her. She had just looked so lovely in the early morning glow, even though she had been covered in dust from head to foot, in a gown that looked as though it needed a thorough wash. The way her eyes had filled with surprise upon seeing him, the way she had whispered so quietly – it had all been utterly enticing, while, of course, he was quite aware she had not meant to present such an alluring picture. And now, he only wanted to kiss her again.

"However," she said, softly, turning to face him. "If you are trying to use me in any way, your grace, then I would ask that you refrain from such actions."

"*Use* you?" he repeated, confused, noticing that she was your-gracing him again.

Her face colored, although she lifted her chin just a little and straightened a bit taller. "Yes, your grace. I'm afraid I heard you discussing certain… thoughts toward… one another with Lord Kenley. Earlier. Olivia and I were on the other side of the potted plant in the drawing room."

A rush of mortification flooded him, searing him from the outside in. He had quite forgotten the sense that someone had overheard them, although he had not seen her. Neither had he taken the opportunity to think about how to explain himself, should he be required to.

"It is not as though I am going to confess my true feelings to *Kenley*!" he blustered, shaking his head. "He is a good friend, of course, but he would rib me endlessly if I declared the truth of my feelings."

"You said that while I was interesting conversation for you and was good company, you had no affection for me but were using me for information, of which I had imparted a great deal," she retorted, in a rote yet accusatory tone. "You are up to something, and to be honest, your grace, I do not want to be toyed with. My stepbrother does quite enough of that, trying to use me for his own intentions to get whatever he pleases. If you truly wish to get close to my stepbrother, then I kindly request that you do so without impinging upon me."

Bradley opened his mouth to refute what she had said, but she was not quite finished.

"I cannot help but think you are playing some kind of *game*," she continued, her entire body growing taut with tension. "Yet I cannot work out what that game is. However, I refuse to play a part in it."

"I play no game," he protested, holding up his hands in

defence of himself. "I swear, Miss Marriott, what I feel for you–"

"Do not say it!" she interrupted, her voice rising. "You are hiding something, and unless you would like to share that with me, I cannot trust anything you say."

He frowned, frustrated that she was laying this at his feet when she herself was also something of an enigma.

"And did you find whatever it was you were looking for, Miss Marriott?" he asked, with a hint of irony in his voice. "Creeping around in the early hours of the morning, covered in dust? I cannot imagine why you would not ask your brother or your staff for help instead of rising before the rest of the house to search for this item."

He saw the way her face paled almost at once, her anger dying away like a cloud going over the sun, leaving in its place a rigid coldness as she shut herself off completely from him.

"This is my house," she said through tight lips. "I can do as I please, and I do not need to explain myself to you."

"But you carry secrets too, I believe," he said, quietly, reaching for her hand in an attempt to make amends. "I do not know what they are, Miss Marriott, and perhaps you do not want to share them."

She stared at him for a few moments, a sheen of tears filling her bright eyes.

"You can talk to me, Miss Marriott," Bradley continued, more softly. "I am a trustworthy man, I swear it."

He drew her closer to him, lowering his head as he bent to kiss those lips that called to him. He felt only air, however, as she wrenched her head back quickly.

"No, you will *not*," she said suddenly, pulling back and stepping away from him. "I will no longer allow myself to be a pawn in your game and you cannot imply that I owe you anything. Do not touch me anymore."

She wrenched her hand from his and turned her back on him. "I have not seen any evidence of your trustworthy nature," she replied hoarsely over her shoulder. "You use me to get close to my stepbrother, and then pretend that I mean something to you. I cannot trust you. My problems will remain my own."

And, with that, she hurried out of the library, leaving the door ajar. Bradley heard a choked sob echo down the hallway, his own heart breaking with the stifled sound.

## CHAPTER 12

Isabella claimed a headache that evening and did not return to the guests until the following day. Her discussion with the duke had rendered her angry, exhausted, and, unfortunately, caused her to shed a tear or two, which was a waste on this situation – a situation she should never have been in to start. She had known better than to form any attachments to a man like the duke.

The next morning she heard a soft knock on her door and opened it to Olivia. Her friend had also heard the duke's words to Lord Kenley and had been livid, ready to charge around the plant and tell the duke exactly what she thought of his words to the earl, but Isabella had asked her not to say anything, choosing to handle it in her own way.

"Are you all right?" she asked Isabella as she sat down on the bed. Isabella was nearly dressed for the day, and dismissed her maid, not wanting her to know of her problems. She chose her jewelry for the evening herself.

"I'm fine, though I feel like such a fool," she said. "I was right to begin with. A man like the duke would never want a woman like me. I was a toy to him, whether for distraction or for some other reason, I do not know. I should have listened to my mind and not my heart."

"Please forgive me, Isabella," said Olivia, her eyes pleading with her. "I truly thought he felt something for you when I encouraged you. Though do you not think, perhaps, he was just putting on a front for Lord Kenley? He looks at you with certainly admiration, though it doesn't excuse what he said. Perhaps give him time to explain himself further."

"No," said Isabella with strength as she slammed shut the jewelry case in front of her and sat at her vanity table. "What I overheard from him as he discussed the matter with Lord Kenley cut much deeper than I ever should have allowed it to. What made it worse was that I must admit that I was beginning to feel something for the duke, despite my best attempts not to. It's all my own fault. I knew better. I should have been smarter."

When he had kissed her, her entire world had come alive, bright and sparkling – only for it all to shatter around her when she had overheard his dismissal of her. Then, seeing him outside her brother's study, the guilt on his face only just masked by his apparent nonchalance, had confused her further. When he had professed his affections for her, she had not known what to believe. And so, her thoughts swirling and heart hurting, she had taken herself to her room, unable to face all of the people awaiting her.

On top of her annoyance at the duke, she was no closer to finding her grandmother's diary. Desperation grew as she lacked the opportunity to search, though she did not share that with Olivia.

"It seems I am unable to discern whether or not the duke was being truly genuine in anything he said, but I must tell you, Olivia, I believe he is hiding something," she said as she rose from her seat. "I found him once leaving the library very early in the morning, and another time in front of Gerard's study, when all the men were to be out riding. I had the distinct impression that he was not telling the truth about what he was doing there."

"Did you not say that Gerard was *also* supposed to be out with the men that afternoon and he remained home?"

"Yes," Isabella frowned, "is that not worse, to compare the duke to my stepbrother?"

Olivia shrugged but seemed to agree with her as she nodded.

"He is obviously using me for something, although what, I just don't know. What on earth am I to believe?"

Olivia looked at her with a smile of confusion herself.

"I'm not sure, Isabella," she said. "But I do know that you deserve happiness, and I truly hope you find it."

"I will," Isabella said with resolve as she thought of the treasure she searched for. "Although quite obviously not with the Duke of Carrington."

Given the confusion that raced through her mind, Isabella decided she wouldn't direct any of her attention toward the duke for the next few days, as she protected her heart instead.

Unfortunately, that seemed to open the door to a persistent Lord Belrose.

She had liked it far better when all of the men had simply left her alone.

* * *

"Might I sit by you for a moment?"

Putting on a smile, and fully aware that she was pale-faced with puffy eyes, Isabella nodded, relieved she had chosen to face away from the window at the afternoon's gathering. She did not want Lord Belrose to ask her anything specific about her well being, for she was quite sure she might burst into tears if he did so – which would go on to cause a great many more problems.

"So," Lord Belrose began, looking as if she had granted him some kind of boon, "might I inquire as to your health?"

Sighing inwardly, Isabella felt her smile become fixed. "I am well, I thank you."

"Your brother told me you had a headache last evening," he replied, looking at her quite earnestly as though he might *see* her headache if he looked hard enough. "Are you recovered, then?"

At that very moment, out of the corner of her eye, Isabella saw the duke glance her way and she caught her breath. Turning a little more to face Lord Belrose, she tried to focus entirely on the man in front of her, not wishing to show the duke any measure of interest.

"Yes, I am recovered, I thank you," she said, softly. "I was just a little tired. I have done too much reading of late. Sometimes I find the stories so interesting I stay up far too late reading by candlelight." She was babbling now, trying to find some way of keeping up a conversation with Lord Belrose, in an effort to dissuade the duke from attempting to talk with her.

"Really?" Lord Belrose asked, his eyes widening as he studied her. "I had no idea you were such an avid reader, Miss Marriott."

"Oh yes," she replied, keeping her gaze fixed on him. "Reading is one of the very great loves of my life, Lord Belrose. I'm afraid I prefer it to almost anything else."

He blinked. "Even to dancing?"

"Yes," she replied, her skin prickling with awareness of the duke drawing nearer, "even to dancing, I'm afraid."

"Well," Lord Belrose exclaimed, sounding quite astonished. "I must confess that I did not know such a thing about you, Miss Marriott. I shall make to purchase a book for you the next time I find myself in a bookshop."

Glancing away from him, Isabella was concerned to see the duke coming within a few steps of them both, an expression of irritation on his face. She did not want to speak to him and certainly did not want to spend any time with him. There was only one thing for it.

"Lord Belrose, another of my great pleasures is to take walks outdoors, although I have not gone out today. Might you escort me? I am quite sure we can gather a few guests for a turn around the gardens." She put a bright smile on her face, hating herself for leading the man on but seeing no other option at the moment. "After all, it is a bright day and not at all cloudy!"

Lord Belrose got to his feet immediately, stammering his agreement and looking at her as though the sun rose and set by her command. Isabella smiled and placed her hand on his arm, not hearing the way he stuttered and stammered his request for other guests to join them for a turn about the grounds. Olivia gave her a questioning look, to which she shrugged in return. Lifting her gaze for the briefest of moments, her eyes locked on the duke's. He looked troubled, even hurt, at her attentions to Lord Belrose, but Isabella could feel nothing but relief.

"Shall we go?" Lord Belrose asked, loudly, a wide grin on his face.

"I must fetch my cloak," Isabella replied, stepping away from him and the duke. "Do excuse me. I will not be but a moment."

* * *

The rest of the day passed in much the same way. Isabella did everything in her power to keep away from the duke, which meant throwing as much attention toward Lord Belrose as possible. Belrose lapped it up, apparently believing that she was slowly warming to him, while Isabella could think of nothing but escaping from the guests and returning to her bedchamber once more.

Even after dinner was completed, there was the usual port for the gentlemen and tea for the ladies, followed by a lively few hours of dancing. Isabella had chosen to play the pianoforte, which meant that she was not required to stand up with anyone – much to the delight of the other ladies, and much to her own relief. The duke chose not to dance at all, standing to the side in conversation, frustrating Lydia and her parents, who tried their best to engage his attentions.

It seemed an age before the entertainments were at an end, but, eventually, she was able to excuse herself and leave the remaining guests to themselves, scurrying up to her room without a moment's hesitation. Before long, she was in her bed, the covers pulled up to her chin. She had not done any searching for the missing diary for two days now, for her mind and heart had been caught up by the duke. Determined that she would continue her search the following day, Isabella closed her eyes and slowly drifted off to sleep.

* * *

"Your grace!"

Turning to see Durand holding a glass out to him, Bradley accepted it with thanks but did not drink, feeling he'd had quite enough already that evening.

"Thank you, Durand." He held the glass carefully in his hand, a warning shooting through him. "How did you enjoy the walk today?" he asked, struggling to think of a way to make conversation.

Durand's eyes flitted from the glass Bradley held to his face. "Yes, yes. It was refreshing, of course." He tried to smile, but there was something hidden just behind his eyes. "If you'll excuse me, however, I think I shall have to retire." He pressed one hand to his head, wincing. "My sister's headaches seem to run in the family!"

"Of course," Bradley replied, quietly, lifting the glass in a small toast. "Good night, Durand. I shall see you come the morning."

Durand nodded and made his way to the door. "Do ensure to keep the good duke company, won't you, Belrose?" he called, seeing the man standing by the decanters. "And top up his brandy when he is finished."

Bradley did not say anything but turned to see Belrose grinning at him, having just poured himself a large measure of brandy. He was tempted to drink his, of course, for it was very fine brandy, but something told him not to touch what Durand had given him. It looked just the same as any normal brandy, and Bradley was quite sure it would taste just the same but, instead of thinking that he was worrying over nothing, he tipped the glass into a nearby potted plant and placed the glass down. He frowned as he saw the froth suddenly bubbling up from the bottom of the glass, as well as from the dampness in the soil of the plant. Had he been right to think that Durand had put something in his brandy? The liquor did not normally fizz and bubble like that.

"Jealous you did not have Isabella all to yourself today, Carrington?"

Bradley did not smile, his thoughts about his brandy flitting away. "I believe it is Miss Marriott to whom you are referring?"

Lord Belrose's smile widened as he swayed a little, the

glass of brandy sloshing in his hand. "Yes, yes, Miss Marriott. Quite the beauty, is she not?"

"Yes," Bradley conceded, sitting down in an armchair beside the fire. "She is." He gazed up at Lord Belrose, both irritated and curious with the fellow. He could not understand why Isabella had seen fit to spend so much time with him today. He had tried, on more than one occasion, to speak to her but she had been far too caught up in conversation, and had even taken a turn about the garden with him. Was she deliberately trying to avoid him? Or did she have some kind of affection for Belrose? The thought made his anger stir, even though it was not Belrose's fault that she bestowed her smile on him.

Lord Belrose chuckled and threw back his brandy in two large gulps, then immediately tottered off to get more.

"Don't you think you've had enough?" Bradley muttered, shaking his head as Charles returned and slumped in the chair opposite, spilling some brandy onto his shirt. "For goodness sake, Belrose, take yourself to bed."

"I am to have her, you know."

Bradley's interest was piqued at once. Perhaps the man's drunkenness was to be to his advantage "Have her? Who are you talking about, man?"

"Isabella, of course," Belrose slurred, "she is to be my wife."

It was as if a lightning bolt struck Bradley, as he felt both hot and cold in equal measure, his skin prickling. "She has accepted you, then?" He had not known that Belrose had even the intention of asking Isabella for her hand and was even more stunned to hear that she had agreed to it.

Lord Belrose chuckled. "Of course."

A shudder ran straight through Bradley, his entire body growing tense. She had agreed to marry Belrose? What on earth had possessed her to do such a thing? Was this her plan to escape her stepbrother?

He did not know what to say, only half listening to Belrose babble on and on about Isabella's great character and how wonderful a wife she would make him. The idea of her married to the man made Bradley almost sick with disappointment, and he was surprised at how strong his feelings were. After all, he had no claim to Isabella, and had he not told himself repeatedly that he was not looking for a wife? Had he not thought that she was nothing more than a distraction from his true cause? Why then had he the sudden urge to shake Lord Belrose until his teeth chattered?

Frowning, Bradley tried to put his thoughts in coherent order but all he could see was Isabella. The way she had responded to his kiss made him believe that she felt nothing for Lord Belrose, and clearly was quite the innocent. Why was it that he could not get her from his mind?

The memory of their kiss had haunted almost every waking moment, as he found that he wanted to do it all over again — and more.

Bradley, however, was not the kind of man who toyed with an innocent lady and took his physical pleasure from her body without any kind of future in mind.

That meant that, should he wish to act on what, until now, had only occurred in his mind, he would seriously have to consider marriage. He was shocked to find that the idea did not send cloying fear to his mind, but rather a peace and quietness. Evidently, he felt more for Miss Marriott than he had allowed himself to admit. But if she was betrothed to Belrose, could he have any kind of hope that she might be easily swayed away from him?

Breaking an engagement would be scandalous, of course, but since it was not yet public, perhaps he had time to sort matters out. First, he would have to win back her trust.

"She will be a most amiable and obedient wife, I am quite sure," Belrose finished, with a grand sweep of his arm. "I am going to be a very happy gentleman."

Bradley shook his head, wondering if Belrose truly knew Isabella. "I confess that I do not think Miss Marriott will be as easily amenable as you think, Belrose." Recalling what he had overheard in the library, Bradley wondered if he might be able to ask the gentlemen more leading questions. It appeared he had something of a loose tongue when he was in his cups.

"She will do as she is told," Belrose said, darkly, making Bradley tense. "That girl has been left to herself for far too long. Her brother wants her fortune, and I want a beautiful wife. All in all, it should work out very nicely. Once we are wed, she will have very little choice but to obey."

Bradley's questions now escaped him as he stared at Belrose in astonishment. He had not thought the man had such a darkness about him, but apparently, it was always carefully hidden. "What do you mean, he wants her wealth?" he asked, attempting casualness. "Is Durand not wealthy already?"

Belrose snorted. "Not nearly as wealthy as his stepsister. Why do you think he lives here?"

"Then how is he to get her wealth for himself?" Bradley asked, most confused. "It is not hers to do with as she pleases?"

His heart went out to the lady, who had clearly found herself in a most unwelcome and untenable situation. There didn't appear to be any love lost between her and her stepbrother and, with no other family to speak of, she evidently was unable to remove him from her home.

"Miss Marriott does not come into her full inheritance until the day of her marriage," Belrose explained, his eyes now half closed. "She has repeatedly refused everyone that her stepbrother has placed in front of her, including me! However, Durand and I have an agreement." He tapped the side of his nose, using the hand that held his brandy glass, which meant that even more liquor fell on to his clothes. However, the man did not seem to notice.

"When she and I are wed, I will give Durand half of her wealth because, of course, as my wife, *her* fortune becomes *my* fortune." He grinned lazily. "After all, we know that women cannot manage money. It will be up to me to do with it as I please."

Bradley clenched his jaw, trying his utmost to keep his temper under control. How dare they use Isabella in such a way?

"Close with Durand, are you?" he muttered, seeing Belrose's eyes slowly begin to close. "Long-time friends?"

"It's the French blood in our veins," Belrose replied, with a large yawn. "It has to count for something, does it not?"

"French blood?" Bradley repeated, trying to pretend he was merely curious. "Whatever does that mean?"

Belrose belched loudly and shook his head. "I am loyal to the Crown," he said, frowning as his eyes glazed over. "Although it is just as well you did not go riding the other day, Carrington. The chap had nefarious intentions for you, I am quite sure."

"Nefarious intentions?" Bradley repeated, trying not to sound too interested. "Do tell me more."

Shrugging, Belrose's eyes became heavy. "Not too sure, but I believe I saw him take something out from under the horse's saddle. The horse that was meant for you, you understand."

"What did he place under it?"

Belrose yawned widely, struggling to keep his eyes open.

"Belrose!" Bradley barked, making the man jerk with surprise. "What did he place under the saddle?"

"Oh, I don't know," Belrose muttered, frustrated. "Looked like a spur of some kind. He was in quite a temper when you decided not to go riding, that's for sure."

Bradley frowned, a sickening, simmering anger beginning in his stomach and slowly rising up through him. Durand had been trying to do away with him? A horse with a spur under its saddle could be unpredictable and Bradley knew he could have easily been thrown should he have gone riding with the rest.

"Best go to my room, old chap," Belrose interrupted, swaying as he attempted to stand. "I'll see you tomorrow."

Bradley wanted to follow him, to grasp him by the collar and shake out more answers, but it seemed it would be futile to do so as Belrose was hardly able to fit two words together.

Instead, Bradley bit his tongue and remained where he was, watching Lord Belrose attempt to make his way to the door.

Doubts lingered in his mind. Something was very wrong about this situation and he did not want to believe Belrose's words without question. Was Isabella really betrothed, as Belrose had said? Or was she merely a pawn in her stepbrother's game, being used in whatever way he wanted?

Bradley shook his head, staring broodily into the fire, knowing that he could not leave the matter to rest. Whether it was his place or not, he would have to speak to Miss Marriott and discover the truth. If she was engaged, as Belrose said, then he would leave things there.

If she was not, however, then he would tell her what he knew. He did not want her to be lured into a marriage with Lord Belrose that would end up hurting her in the end.

But if he said anything to the contrary, would she speak to him? Would she believe him?

His eyes went to the plant where he had poured his brandy and, to his utter shock, he saw that the leaves were wilting, yellowing. Had he been correct? Had Durand put something in his glass? A slight shudder went through him as he rose from his chair, picked up the offending glass, and threw it in the fire.

This had all suddenly taken on a more dangerous turn.

## CHAPTER 13

The next night, Isabella padded down the hallway with the candlestick held firmly in her hand, trying so hard to be quiet that she nearly didn't breathe as she climbed the staircase to the upper floor of the estate. Gerard and the rest of his guests were still awake, judging by the sound of the raucous laughter that floated up to her. It had been another day of evading the duke, and tonight she had managed to slip away almost unnoticed, not having any particular interest in either playing cards or joining in the ribald conversation.

Sighing to herself, she shook her head and leaned against the wall for a moment, taking a breath after the swiftness of her climb. She would be well hidden from Gerard and the other guests by now. Even if they did come out of the drawing room to make their way to their beds, they would not see her. She intended to spend a few hours searching some of the smaller, unused rooms at the top of the house. All the bedchambers were on the floor below, which meant that no one had any reason to be up here.

She walked down the slightly eerie corridor. This floor

was so rarely used, it had an empty, lonely feel to it. She approached the door of the room she wanted to search, which she remembered as a long, open room that had always been used to store various items.

Once she was within, the light of her candlestick would not be seen through the solid oak door. Pushing it with all her might, she prayed that it would open, her grip turning the handle of the door but, to her frustration, it did not budge. Setting the candlestick down, she tried the door handle again, feeling it turn completely. It was just her strength that was lacking then, for it was evident the door was unlocked, but stuck. Gerard had stolen her keys to the house some time ago, and she had never been able to retrieve all of them so the fact that these doors remained unlocked was a blessing.

"Might I help you?"

A low voice had her shrieking, the sound echoing through the corridors. Clapping a hand over her mouth, she turned to see none other than the duke approach her, his eyes on her face. A sudden weakness rushed through her from the fright he had given her and she sagged against the door, only for him to catch her under the elbow.

"I do apologize, Miss Marriott," he said, quietly. "I did not mean to startle you."

"Hush, please!" she exclaimed, wrenching her arm from his. She waited until he had clamped his mouth shut before listening hard for any change in the sounds from the other guests. Thankfully, the laughter was still the same, and someone was hammering out some awful tune on the pianoforte. Letting out a long sigh of relief, Isabella glared at the duke, hating that he had somehow discovered her presence up here.

"I confess I followed you," he continued, as though

reading her thoughts. "We have not spoken in almost two days and I could not continue in such a fashion."

"Please," Isabella begged, keeping her voice as low as possible. "You must be quiet. I cannot be seen here."

He studied her for a moment, before nodding and stepping forward toward the door she had been trying to open. He had to put his shoulder to it, but soon the door began to move, creaking loudly as it opened to them. Once there was a big enough gap for her to escape through, Isabella nipped inside, holding her candlestick aloft so that she might look about the room.

The duke's presence behind her made her catch her breath despite herself, her heart leaping into her throat as his arm grazed hers.

"Here," he said gruffly, holding out another candlestick. "This room could do with a little more light."

"I am not sure they will take," Isabella replied, frowning. "This room looks to have remained unused for some time." The candles sputtered and refused to catch but, eventually, they did and the duke took both three-pronged candlesticks from her, holding them aloft. It certainly helped her to see the room a little more clearly. It was full of old furniture and forgotten belongings, most covered by cloth and dust.

"I do not require any further assistance, your grace," she said, turning to the duke.

"Carrington," he corrected her.

"Your grace," she repeated. "Although I do thank you for your help thus far."

His brows furrowed as his blue eyes bore into hers with an intensity that made her tingle. "Oh no, Miss Marriott. I am not about to be so easily sent away. I believe we have much to say to each other."

She frowned and looked down, cursing her own reaction

to him despite how she tried to keep him away. "I do not believe I have anything to say to you, your grace."

"I think you do." Putting the candlestick down on a dusty covered table, he moved closer to her and caught her chin with one gentle finger. Raising her face to his, he waited until she met his gaze before speaking. There was a softness in his expression that made her heart quicken its pace and her entire body come alive at once.

She tried to remain quite stern faced toward him, but it did not take much, it seemed, for her to fall back under his spell, despite her inclination not to do so. Her foolish heart was already twined with his, even though she had promised herself not to consider him any longer.

"I am here to help you, Miss Marriott," he said, quietly. "I will be honest with you if you can be honest with me."

Surprised, she regarded him with caution. "You mean to say that you will tell me what it is you have been hiding? I was right to suspect so?"

"You are quite right, Miss Marriott," he replied, sounding resigned to the fact that he would have to reveal all in order for her to trust him. "I have been hiding the truth from you, but no longer."

Isabella did not know what to think. Should she believe him and tell him everything that was going on? Did he truly wish to help her?

"I can go first if you prefer," he said, softly, with a half-smile. "I have been untrustworthy up until this point, but no longer. I swear it. You deserve the truth, and not just because I want to prove myself to you."

Isabella nodded, and sat down in an old dusty chair, not caring about her gown. "Very well," she said, gesturing for him to begin. He looked a trifle uncomfortable as he took a seat across from her in a matching chair that had been hidden away for storage and seemingly forgotten. He began to speak, warning her that what he had to say might not be easily accepted on her part, but still, he continued. Hearing about his friend's death, Isabella's heart wrenched, her hand going to her chest at the pain on his face as he described the man who had been his closest friend.

"And so, you think my stepbrother might be the man behind all this," she said slowly, narrowing her eyes a little.

The duke shrugged. "I cannot say for certain, Miss Marriott. All I know is that there are three Frenchmen here and two of them are in league with one another, although Belrose is not privy to all that Gerard has planned."

Isabella stared at him in shock. "*Lord Belrose* is the one involved with my brother?"

He cleared his throat and nodded, looking a little abashed. "I am afraid that Charles Belrose is a little too talkative when he is in his cups. He explained to me that your stepbrother has promised you to him on the condition that, once you are wed, he gives half of your fortune to Durand."

A cold chill washed over her at his words, her heart sinking to the floor. She had known that Gerard had a nefarious plot planned for her, but she had not considered that he would go to such lengths.

"I see," she said, through numb lips.

"I am sorry to have to tell you this about your betrothed, but I felt you should know."

"My betrothed?" Her head snapped toward him in surprise. "I am not betrothed to the man, your grace."

"According to Lord Belrose and your stepbrother, you are."

She gave a harsh laugh that echoed strangely off the walls, bare of all but dust and grime. "I have never liked my stepbrother, your grace. I believe you can see why."

"He has moved here without your consent," the duke said

matter-of-factly, as some relief showed on his face. "And you have no one to aid you."

"Indeed," Isabella whispered, hanging her head. "Well, that is somewhat untrue. I do have Olivia, though she does not know the full extent of the goings-on here." She smiled through the tears that threatened to fall due to her frustration at the entire situation. She rapidly blinked them back "She was quite put out by your actions the other day, your grace. You are lucky I held her back."

A sudden thought struck her and she looked up at him, terrified that he would think her complicit. "You do not think that I am in any way *involved* in this scheme?"

"No, of course not," he reassured her, his words filled with sincerity. "Well — I admit I did wonder at first, but not once I came to know you better. Though I could tell from the first moment I met you that you did not care for your brother. It has not been until I came here that I discovered the full truth about what he is like."

Isabella dropped her head, trying desperately to keep her tears at bay. She did not want to break down in front of him, but she had been forced to be so strong for such a great length of time that even just speaking with him about this made her carefully constructed walls begin to crumble.

His hand lightly touched her shoulder and she looked up to see the duke looking down at her with a sympathetic smile. "I am here to help you, Miss Marriott, if you will let me," he said, with a tenderness that made her want to weep. "I confess that I have a growing affection for you which, for my own reasons, I have been battling but, regardless of whether you return them or not, I wish to help you in your current predicament."

Isabella swallowed the lump in her throat and gave him a somewhat watery smile. "I confess that my thoughts are so confused that I am not sure in what direction to turn."

"Then tell me what it is you are searching for," he said, crouching down in front of her so that he might look more deeply into her eyes. "I know that you have not found it, whatever it is, as you told me."

"No, I have not," Isabella replied, miserably. Haltingly, she began to tell him a few details, but then found herself relating to him the whole story, including her plan to run away to the Americas. She thought he might laugh at her for being so ridiculous but, instead, he simply nodded.

"Quite a predicament we are in, then," he murmured, with a smile tugging at the corner of his mouth. "Both searching for something we cannot be sure is here."

Isabella tried to laugh but could not quite manage it, her emotions so close to the surface that she was struggling to contain them. "You need to open the cabinet drawers, then," she said, softly. "I am sure I know where he hides the key, although we will have to find a way into the study again."

"It was not locked the last time," he replied, with a frown. "Is that unusual?"

"Very," Isabella replied, firmly. "Perhaps it was because he knew he was not to go riding after all and all of the guests were out." Her eyes searched his face, realizing that, for the first time, there was a frankness about his expression that told her he was being completely honest with her. She could not be angry over his lack of willingness to discuss the situation, given what he suspected of her stepbrother, but the knowledge that she might not only be related to, but housing, a traitor brought cold shame to her heart. She would help him if, for no other reason, than to determine Gerard's true nature.

"Perhaps we might go in the dead of night," he suggested, chuckling at her surprised expression. "Lord Kenley is, in fact, something of a genius when it comes to locks, although I think the locks in the cabinet are too small for even his nimble fingers. We shall require the key for those ones, I believe."

Isabella gave a slow smile. "I know where that key is hidden."

"Wonderful," the duke smiled, pressing her hand for a moment. "Then we shall see for certain whether or not your brother is the one behind Roger's murder." His smile slipped. "And if he is, then I am sorry for whatever consequences come your way, even though you will have nothing to do with the situation."

"Please," she replied, grasping his hand firmly. "You must not worry about me. I will have my freedom in either case and that is the most important thing to me."

Their eyes met and their gazes held for what felt like minutes, to the point that Isabella felt her heart slam into her chest repeatedly, suddenly overwhelmed by what she saw in his eyes. Shadows flickered across his face from the candlelight, highlighting his dark eyes and strong jaw brushed with stubble, and the memory of his lips on hers returned forcefully to her mind.

"Miss Marriott," he breathed, his words caressing her cheek. "I am sorry for what I have done to cause you pain and confusion. Believe me when I say that you are the most beautiful woman I've ever laid eyes upon and that, despite my embittered heart, I am discovering that I cannot fight myself any longer when it comes to you."

Isabella inhaled swiftly at his revelation. But that was only the beginning. He continued.

"I want you more than I have ever wanted anything before in my life."

## CHAPTER 14

*S*he could not speak, had no ready response, and when his mouth pressed against hers in a searing kiss, it was all she could do to hold onto him, desperate for him to linger. Fire erupted deep within her, shooting flames through her whole body as he angled his head to deepen the kiss. Her arms made their way around his neck, her fingers digging into the silky dark chestnut of his hair as she clung to him. There was no help for her. Her strength of mind was too weak, she thought, as her mouth parted beneath the insistent pressure of his. Or maybe her heart was too strong.

She drew in a shuddering breath as he dragged his lips from hers and began to kiss a trail down her neck. Stunned, she realized that his hand was on the curve of her breast, burning through the thin cotton of her dress. She ought to be fighting it, ought to be telling him to stop, but Isabella discovered her body was reacting in ways she had never experienced before. Nerves mingled with desire, her breath coming hard.

He lifted his head and smiled at her, dark passion within

his glittering blue eyes. She looked back at him, her pulse thundering in her ears. Her gaze flicked to his mouth, aware of where it had been only moments before. Involuntary tremors raked her body as he brushed the tips of his fingers across her breast, making her gasp. Then, his mouth was back on hers once more, and she was just as helpless to stop him.

He caught her around the waist, pressing her hard against the wall so that the length of his body was flush against hers. Something pressed against her belly and, immediately, desire raced through her — a longing for something she did not quite understand. Heat pooled in her core, making its way down her body, and Isabella flushed with embarrassment, gasping against the onslaught of his lips.

He broke the kiss and gently pushed down the bodice of her dress, freeing her breasts. His eyes roved over them, before his lips trailed down along her neck to the rosy bud of her nipple. She gasped as he sucked it, his fingers toying with the other side. His lips returned to hers as his wide hands spanned her waist, while her arms wrapped around him and her fingers dug into his back and bicep.

She moaned, and the sound must have brought him back to his senses for suddenly he was gone, holding her at arm's length.

"I must apologize," he muttered, suddenly breaking their connection and drawing in a ragged breath as he rested his forehead against hers. "I should not be taking such liberties. Forgive me."

Isabella found that she had no words, her body still roaring with heat, her blood still pumping through her with a ferocity she had not expected.

"It is not... that is I... I *welcomed* it. Do not be sorry."

"I suppose we should begin our search," he said, with just

a hint of laughter in his words as he stroked her cheek. "My dear Miss Marriott, you are too tempting for words."

"Isabella," she gasped out.

His eyes widened. "Isabella, then. Could we revisit Bradley?"

She looked up at him with some trepidation. "Perhaps when — when we are alone."

He gave her a wolfish grin as he let her go, easing her away from him, his fingers lingering on hers as he led her to the middle of the room where they began exploring. It was eerily quiet here, seemingly another house entirely.

Isabella tried to refocus on the search, relieved to no longer be alone in her quest but unable to focus on what she was looking for. Her body had responded to his kisses, while her mind was in torment over him. She wanted to explore things further, wondering if he could satisfy this urgent, desperate need he had awakened in her, but knowing that it was quite foolish to suggest it.

For heaven's sake, she could be ruined if someone saw her even kissing the man! Though did it matter? She was planning to leave anyway, far away from England where no one would know anything about her. That was, unless he was genuine in his affections, for then her future could look quite different. Did he mean what he said? Could she trust that, despite their difference in status, in wealth, and even in life, that he might truly hold some affection for her?

His willingness to help her, his encouragement to speak openly of all the difficulties she faced, told her that he did truly feel for her and wanted to assist her in her troubles. He could have very easily walked away from her and focused only on his task, but instead here he was.

*Or was it because she knew where the key was?*

The inner voice of caution rose up within her. Isabella shook her head to herself, refusing to believe what it told her. The duke — Bradley — had been honest enough to tell her all of his secrets, which included the potential treason her brother was involved in. He would not have told her the extent of it if he did not trust her. What she did not know was the depths of his affection. He could very easily breeze in and out of her life, with only a few stolen kisses and whispered words as memories of their time together.

Seeing him glance over at her, and aware that she was standing quite still instead of searching, Isabella turned to the next lot of shelves and began to hunt for the diary.

She had to be more careful – or she might lose her heart entirely.

* * *

THEIR SEARCH YIELDED NOTHING, and finally, as Isabella yawned and weaved where she was standing, the duke declared it was time to get some sleep. He led Isabella out the door and back down the stairs, where the house was now quiet. He bid her goodnight at her door before hurrying away to his own room as though by slowing down he would tempt himself to remain.

Isabella was tempted herself. She wanted to ask him to come into her chamber, but she wasn't sure if she was ready to give herself to a man who may not be part of her future.

Changing out of her dusty gown and into her nightclothes, Isabella was so tired that despite her racing thoughts, she soon fell into a deep sleep. When she woke hours later, it was still pitch black outside and she was befuddled as to what had awakened her, until she heard the noise.

It was shouting — or a moan? She couldn't be sure, but it seemed to be coming from the room next door, which would be the duke's bedchamber. Had Gerard entered his room — was he trying to do something to him? Sudden worries about the duke had Isabella flying from her bed, not considering how she was dressed – or undressed. She scrambled for the key to unlock the door of the adjoining dressing room, and she found the door on the duke's side still unlocked.

She pushed open the door, unsure of what she would find. When she stepped into his room, however, the only person within was the duke himself. He was tossing and turning in his bed, mumbling and moaning in his sleep.

Before she could think of what she was doing, Isabella crossed to the bed, gently nudging his shoulder. When that didn't do anything, she shook his arm, hard, in an attempt to wake him. Still, his arms flailed, and she had to duck to keep from him hitting her in his sleep. Finally she grabbed him by the shoulders and called out to him — "Carrington! Carrington! Bradley!"

His eyes flew open and he immediately stilled, taking in his surroundings and Isabella's face.

"Isabella? I — what... what are you doing?"

"You were shouting out in your sleep. I came to see what was the matter."

"Oh," he said, looking equal parts relieved and distressed. "I'm sorry to have disturbed you. It's nothing."

"Clearly it is *something*," she said, incredulous. "You were quite distraught."

"It's only a dream," he said, not looking at her but over her shoulder, into the distance. "A nightmare really, that visits me over and over again. I dream of Roger's death, the bullet coming through the air and striking him in the chest as he sat on the horse beside me."

"Oh," she said as she lifted a hand to his face. "I'm so sorry."

"Nothing to be sorry for," he said, his face softening as she leaned over him. "The dreams have lessened since I've been here, actually — since I met you."

She blushed, and then looked around her as if suddenly realizing when and where she was.

"I... I should probably return to my room."

"You probably should."

But for some reason she could not pull herself away from him, as she stayed, leaning down over him. Slowly, she lowered her face to his, kissing him so softly, so sweetly that she barely felt his lips.

He reached his hand up into her hair, loosening it from its braid as he twined his fingers through it and let it fall down her back. He lifted her from where she sat on the edge of the bed and placed her on top of him, deepening the kiss and running his hands down her body. She felt every touch of him through her thin nightgown, and her skin was on fire everywhere his fingers had been.

She lifted her mouth from his. "I want... I need..." she whispered to him, as she yearned for something she couldn't put words to.

"I know darling, but I won't do that to you, not yet," he said, as much as it pained him, "though I long to as well."

She touched her forehead to his, knowing he was right but not willing to accept it. "I just... you make something come alive inside me, that I never knew was possible."

She kissed him again, hoping that it would help douse the fire that was burning so hotly, but instead it only served to fuel it.

His fingers went to the bottom of her nightgown, and he slowly inched them up her leg. She opened to him, knowing if not what to do then at least what she needed, and when he found her most tender place, she arched up at a sensation unlike anything she had never felt before. His fingers moved over her nub, as the ache built within her.

"Please," she said, not knowing what she was asking for.

He did, however. He flipped her over so she was underneath him, and he trailed kisses down her body as he moved lower.

"What… what are you doing?" she asked. "You can't —"

"I can," he said, as his tongue replaced his fingertips, and he brought her the satisfaction she had been longing for.

# CHAPTER 15

Despite the very-welcome visit from Isabella the previous night, Bradley spent the following day feeling nothing but tension, aware that he would, very soon, be at the climax of his investigation. He was more and more certain that Durand was the man behind Roger's death, given that he now believed that Durand had attempted to create a situation where it would appear that Bradley had been the victim of a tragic accident.

Of course, Belrose could be quite mistaken about what he had seen, and Bradley might have no reason to be on his guard but, regardless, he could not help his edginess. Visions of what Gerard might do assailed him. Poison in his teacup, a sudden shove over the side of the stairs. Of course, he did not think that Durand would do something so obvious, for these would, no doubt, place suspicion on both himself and his guests. If Durand did plan for Bradley's death, then it would have to either look like an accident or be far away from the Durand estate, as the ambush on him and Roger had been.

"Ready?"

Bradley frowned as his friend extricated himself from the dancers to make his way over to him. "You sound much too eager, Kenley."

"That is only because I am excited about what we might find," Alastair replied with a grin. "While you have been chasing evidence as well as Miss Marriott, I have done nearly nothing at all. I have had to act just as any other guest might."

Shaking his head, Bradley couldn't help but grin at his friend's wry expression. "And you have enjoyed every minute of it. Dancing, cards, liquor, Lady Olivia… you cannot tell me that you have found that a trial!"

Alastair laughed. "I cannot hide the truth from you, Carrington."

"No, indeed, you cannot," Bradley agreed, fervently. "I am sorry for what I said about Miss Marriott, however. It has taken me some time to accept my attraction to her… and even longer to consider what else might come from it."

His friend did not look in the least bit surprised. "Indeed. I must say that I am glad to see your cynical heart has found its match at last, Carrington. She will be good for you."

"I am not about to propose, Kenley!" Bradley exclaimed, slightly flustered. "I mean, we have– "

"Why ever not?" Alastair interrupted, lifting one eyebrow. "You are well suited, you quite obviously lust after her and you clearly have an affection for each other which, in time, I'm quite sure will turn to love, and you shall have the kind of marriage most of us can only dream of."

"I…." Bradley tried to think of some reason as to why he would not consider matrimony to Isabella. Perhaps Alastair was right. He made it sound so simple. If Gerard was guilty, there would be some scandal, but Bradley didn't care so much about that.

"At least let us get this entire business out of the way first," he said, eventually. "Then we shall see where the path takes us."

Alastair chuckled. "It might take us to the end of your investigation, Carrington. Then what shall you do?"

It was on the tip of Bradley's tongue to say that he would help Miss Marriott to find her family's heirloom so that she might be free of her stepbrother for good, but he realized first that it was her secret to tell and secondly, the thought of wedding her would not escape him.

If he married her, then she could seek the heirlooms still but with no urgent need pushing her to continue searching with such desperation. They had not found anything last evening and he had seen the worry on her face as they had closed the door to the second room, evidently growing more concerned that, without the box, she was destined to be used as part of her stepbrother's cruel schemes whether she wished it or not.

"Ah, Miss Marriott," he murmured, when the woman in his thoughts drew closer to them as the rest of the guests continued with their dancing. "How lovely you look this evening."

She smiled, as two spots of red appeared in her cheeks, adding to her loveliness. Tonight she was dressed in pale-yellow which reminded him of sunshine, with delicate lace around the bodice that he longed to remove once again. "Thank you, your grace."

"Please," he said, quietly. "Bradley." He chuckled, seeing the way she glanced at him in surprise, as Lord Kenley stood with them. He had so many secrets — he didn't want another with her. "I believe I have told you, on more than one occasion, that I am not a stickler for propriety."

Lord Kenley excused himself and suddenly became very interested in the painting next to them.

Bradley's heart swelled as he thought of more private

times with her, and he caught her hand, pressing a light kiss on the back of it.

"Isabella," he whispered. Her name on his lips felt right, as though it belonged there. "I need your help with something. Something regarding the plots I suspect your brother of. I shall retire to my room and, if you wish to join me, will meet you shortly."

Her blush deepened, but she nodded and moved away from him, walking over to her stepbrother and begging to excuse herself. Bradley chuckled to himself on seeing how she put on a pained expression, pressing one hand to her head. The excuse of a headache was to be used again, and, evidently, Gerard Durand did not care for it, excusing her with a brisk wave of his hand and a disgruntled expression on his face. Bradley waited for another half hour before taking his leave of the guests – but not before he caught Lord Belrose shooting worried glances his way. Had the man recalled what he had said to Bradley in his drunken state?

As soon as he was back in his bedchamber, he opened the door to the small dressing room and found Isabella standing there, looking a little lost.

"Well done," he smiled, stepping forward and catching her in his arms. "I cannot tell you how pleased I am that you've arrived. I am quite sure this will all be over soon, and you will be free of your stepbrother regardless of what we find."

"But we did not find the diary, and I'm not sure where else to search," she murmured as she stepped back, her eyes not quite meeting his. "If Gerard is not guilty, then I cannot be free unless I find it."

The urge to tell her that he could give her that freedom came over him with such strength that he had to bite his lip to keep the words back. Now was not the time nor the place to propose, for he had not even sorted the idea out in his own mind.

"I said I would keep you safe from him," he said instead eventually, his arms going around her waist as he tugged her to him, wishing he could protect her from her stepbrother just by keeping her in his arms forever. "And I meant it, Isabella. You need have no fear where your stepbrother is concerned. Please… trust me."

Her eyes met his and slowly the concern left them, and he felt the expulsion of her long breath on his neck. "I do trust you," she whispered, the smallest of smiles catching her lips. "I'm not sure exactly why, but I do."

He could do nothing but kiss her gently, feeling the stirring in his loins that warned him not to take things too far. She was vulnerable and he did not want to take advantage of that. However, he couldn't seem to hold himself back completely, finding his hand drifting to brush the soft skin above the neckline of her dress.

His mouth slanted over hers as his tongue skimmed her lips. She opened to him, catching his bottom lip with her teeth, driving him mad.

His hunger for her increased with her own persistence and he lifted her knee up around his hip, pressing against her. He unconsciously began to lift up at her skirts, drinking in her gasp. She lifted her mouth and moaned into his ear — and it was only when the sound of his bedchamber door opening met his ears that she pushed back, looking up at him with shock in her eyes.

He smiled at her, her hair mussed and her mouth red after his thorough kiss. He lifted her dress back up over her exposed breasts.

"Just Lord Kenley," he whispered, dropping a kiss on her forehead. He reluctantly released her and led her back to his room.

Alastair did not look in the least bit surprised to discover that the two had been ensconced together, although he sent an obvious wink Bradley's way.

"And now we must be patient," Bradley declared, ignoring Alastair altogether. "We shall have to wait until all are abed."

"They were all retiring as I left," Alastair said, settling himself in a chair by the hearth. "I asked for a tray to be sent up to your room."

Bradley nodded. He had not eaten much at dinner, given his focus on what was to come that evening, and a tea tray sounded just the thing.

"Very good, Kenley," he said, as Isabella sat down opposite his friend. "I doubt any of us will be able to sleep while we wait, although do not let me stop you from resting."

"No, indeed," Isabella declared, smiling at them both, although Bradley could see the strain in her expression. "I feel so anxious that I am not sure I could sleep a wink, even if I tried."

"Courage, Miss Marriott," Alastair smiled, as there came a knock on the door. "By this time tomorrow evening, all will be in order."

Bradley rose to open the door as Isabella hid behind it so as not to give herself away to the servants. Bradley's eyes widened in surprise as he opened it to find not the butler, nor a footman, but instead a very blonde, very beautiful, very bemused woman.

# CHAPTER 16

"Lady Olivia!" he said in surprise, as the woman pushed past him into the room. "I say, I'm not sure—"

She looked around the room, taking in Isabella behind the door, a shocked expression on her face, and Alastair in front of the hearth with a grin stretching from ear to ear. He rose, lifted her hand in his, and placed a kiss on the back of it.

"Anger becomes you, milady," he said, obviously raising her ire even further.

She lifted her eyebrows as the three of them looked at her like schoolchildren caught by the headmistress.

"At first, it was fairly clear what was happening when the two of you disappeared early," she said to Bradley and Isabella before pointing at Alastair. "But *you*, my lord, are not known to withdraw from entertainment until the very end of the evening. Now, who will tell me what is happening here?"

Bradley looked to Isabella, who seemed at a loss. She nodded to him that he could trust Lady Olivia, but she looked seriously at her friend.

"Olivia," she said slowly. "What we speak about must not leave this room."

"Do you not trust me?" said Lady Olivia indignantly.

"Olivia."

"All right, I realize that I'm not known for discretion," she said, waving a hand in the air as she rolled her eyes. "But if this is truly important, I promise I will not say a word."

He was not quite convinced, but Bradley saw no other option and shared an outline of the details of what had brought them together. Lady Olivia looked enthralled at the thought of being involved in such intrigue. He begged her to return to her room — four of them could be too much of a crowd — but she refused, now too excited to let this continue without her.

An hour or so later, Bradley caught the look on Alastair's face, stopped his pacing, and glanced at the clock.

"I think now we should be all right," he said, walking toward the door. "Give me a moment to check that the way is clear."

Opening the door just a crack, Bradley listened carefully for any sounds, only to be thoroughly convinced that the rest of the party had, finally, chosen to retire. There was no laughter, no tinkling of the piano. Instead, there was only the beautiful sound of silence.

"Come then," he whispered, holding his hand out to Isabella. "We must go."

"What about the candle?" Alastair asked, holding up a single candlestick. "We will be quite lost without a light."

Bradley nodded and held out his hand for it and, together, the four of them walked along the quiet corridor down to the study.

"We must go down the stairs," Isabella whispered, her hand tightening in Bradley's grip. "But they do creak terribly."

He nodded but said nothing, letting go of her hand and slowly beginning to descend the staircase. With every sound, he cringed, quite sure that Durand would throw open his bedchamber door and come hurtling down the hall to see what they were doing, but, to his very great relief, they reached the bottom without incident.

Bradley reached for Isabella's hand once more, appreciating the way her fingers twined with his. He was just about to make his way forward once more when Isabella gave a slight tug and put a finger to her lips. Bradley froze, holding the candle low in the hope that, should someone be walking around, they would not see it. There was the briefest of scuffling sounds, and, to his horror, the sound of a door being opened.

Isabella moved at once, practically dragging him forward with Alastair and Lady Olivia close behind. Together he and Isabella slipped into an alcove, and, worried they would be found, Bradley blew out the candle.

The moonlight through the windows cast an eerie shadow across the hallway, highlighting the various portraits on the wall opposite. Bradley tried not to react to the way Isabella pressed herself against him, but could not help but wrap an arm around her waist to draw her closer.

He saw Alastair was now across the hallway, crouching behind a large marble statue with Lady Olivia behind his back, but there did not seem to be any further sounds to suggest someone was coming. In fact, the house returned to its quiet state once more, causing Bradley to let out a long, slow breath of relief.

"Can you still force the lock without a light?" he whispered to Alastair as they began to move slowly to the study. They could not see where they were going particularly well, and their progress was slow.

"I should be able to," Alastair replied, calmly. "And if not, I shall simply send you back to your bedchamber to fetch another candle."

Bradley did not smile, despite Alastair's attempt at mirth, worried about the progress of their investigation. Finally making it to the door of the study, he tried the handle but found that it was, as Isabella had predicted, firmly locked.

Alastair, however, was not put off in the least. Bending down, he pulled two metal tools from his pocket and began poking away at the lock. He had been quite mischievous in his youth, a trait that had not left him.

Bradley had no idea what the man was doing, but instead stood anxiously beside the door, putting one arm around Isabella's shoulders as they waited. They simply could not be discovered for, if they were, then any evidence that might be within could simply be disposed of by Gerard.

A sudden click made him tense, and he heard Alastair's sharp intake of breath. He saw him turn the handle and, to his very great delight, the door swung open. Within seconds they were all inside, and the door finally closed.

Letting out a long breath, Bradley saw that a tiny flame still flickered in a spent candle and, with haste, he rushed to light another. It caught at once and he handed it to Isabella, who carefully circled Gerard's desk.

"This desk was my father's," she said, softly. "As was the cabinet. I know that my father often kept a spare key hidden in the underside of one of these drawers…but I cannot quite remember which one."

"Take your time," Bradley replied, despite his racing heart. He waited with growing impatience as she continued to search, praying that the spare key would be there. A soft cry met his ears as, to his relief, she rose with a grin on her face, holding the smallest of keys.

Bradley wanted to kiss her then and there but just managed to prevent himself from doing so. Instead, he crushed her to him for a moment, murmuring a "well done" into her ear, before Alastair cleared his throat and urged him not to waste any more time, as he directed Lady Olivia to keep watch on the door.

Alastair held aside the curtain as Bradley opened the cabinet door. The drawers were still there and still locked tightly. This was the moment he would discover whether or not Gerard Durand was the man behind Roger's death – and whether he was truly seeking to do away with Bradley himself. The key found the lock and slid in at once, turning neatly and quietly. A soft click told him the top drawer was open, but Bradley did not pull out the contents.

Instead, he opened all three drawers and then handed the key back to Isabella, who moved to put it away. Then, he opened the top drawer and, seeing the parchments and documents, picked them up as one and handed them to Alastair. The second drawer's contents went to Isabella and the third drawer he took for himself.

"Now," he said, bending down to spread out the parchments on the carpet and calling softly to Lady Olivia to come help them. "Look carefully, each of you. Any evidence of ties to France, and of treason to the Crown, is what we are looking for."

They all nodded their understanding.

"Hurry."

## CHAPTER 17

Isabella could not see the documents she held particularly well, so hastened to light another two candles, returning to hand one to Lord Kenley before looking through her own pile of papers. Her heart began racing as she began her search, not sure whether or not she truly wished to find something.

If Gerard was a traitor to England, if he had been the one who had killed Roger and had tried to kill Bradley, then his neck would likely be stretched by the noose within weeks, were he arrested. Shuddering, she put yet another note filled with numbers and monies to one side.

"Wait."

Her voice was a whisper, but her three companions were by her side within seconds. With a hand that shook slightly, she picked up what appeared to be a bundle of letters, but with French writing on the front.

"I cannot read French," Bradley admitted, gruffly. "What does it say, Isabella?"

She swallowed once and pulled the first letter from the ribbons, unfolding it carefully. It did not appear to be too old, and she was able to read the words with ease. Her breath came a little more easily as she realized there was nothing untoward about the letter.

"There are just some greetings, and the like," she said, quietly. "Gerard has many friends still in Paris, of course. It is quite right that they should keep in correspondence, although…" She frowned, trying to recall whether or not she knew the writer of the letter. "I cannot say if I knew this Vaquelin, however, and I thought I had met each of Gerard's acquaintances on at least one occasion when we lived in France."

"Here," Bradley murmured, pulling another letter from the pile, but, this time, closer to the middle. "We cannot take any chances. What does this one say?"

Isabella unfolded it carefully, only for her eyes to widen as she began to read the words within.

"I have heard there are men within your society who are searching for you. Our relationship cannot continue for as long as they hunt," she read, her voice growing hoarse. "Your notes on some of England's weaknesses are thorough but you must be on your guard. France will have the victory!"

There was a long silence. Isabella stared down at the parchment in her hand, aware that she held the evidence that meant Gerard would be sent to jail for treason.

"My goodness," Lord Kenley whispered after Isabella shared the information. "You were right to suspect him, Carrington."

"It does not tell us what relationship he has with this man, nor why it was important," Bradley replied impatiently. "But I do not think that now is either the time or the place to begin looking into such things. We must take these letters with us and I will return to London at once."

Isabella rose and stood beside Olivia with an icy hand wrapped around her heart. For all that she had disliked her stepbrother, she had never thought of him being executed, though she knew it was the only fair consequence for what he had chosen to do. He could have returned to France and lived there quite peacefully, if he had such a loyalty to the country – but to come to England, to use her to access society, and then to search out its weak spots to pass onto those in France who wished to mount an attack was quite horrifying.

"I'm sorry, Isabella," Olivia whispered to her, with a hand on her back in comfort.

Isabella raised her head stoically and looked at her friend. "I cannot feel sorry for him," she said, her jaw set firmly. "Whatever are the consequences of his actions, he has brought them upon himself."

Olivia nodded, though Isabella knew it was not Gerard she felt sorry for, but her. Any prospects she might have had would likely disappear altogether, as the stepsister of a traitor. She didn't really care about any such prospects, however... except for one.

"Come now." Bradley took her hand and together, they walked toward the study door. She glanced behind her, seeing everything back in its proper place.

"The only thing we cannot do is lock the door," Kenley whispered, frowning. "But that cannot be helped."

Isabella nodded and entered the hallway – only to pause mid-step, catching Bradley's arm. "Wait," she whispered, as Kenley shut the study door and came to stand next to them and Olivia. "Is that not a carriage?"

The front door to the estate was not far from where they stood and, as one, they flew toward it. It was ajar and, to her horror, she saw Belrose's carriage trundle past them, before heading for the gate. Apparently, Charles Belrose was running away.

"We must go after him," Bradley said, quickly handing

Isabella the stack of letters. "Read these, Isabella. Discover what you can. I will return later today with the men I need to arrest your brother. Please, stay with all of the other guests until I return?"

Isabella looked up at him, only able to make out his features by the dim morning light. "I intend to feign ignorance for as long as I can."

He brushed her cheek with his fingers. "I know this is difficult for you, love," he said, a little more softly. "But all shall be put to rights by the end of the day, I assure you. You will be free and quite safe, I promise."

She gave him a quick forced smile and nodded, her eyes dropping to the stack of letters in her hand. "I will look for your return."

His mouth was on hers just as soon as she finished speaking, ignoring the presence of Olivia and Lord Kenley altogether. It was hot and sweet, a kiss that spoke of promise and hope – and then, in the next moment, he was gone from her side. She kept her eyes on him for as long as she could, only to see him and Lord Kenley disappear into the darkness. Closing the door quietly, she leaned against it for a moment, shutting her eyes and letting the severity of tonight's events sink into her mind.

"Oh Isabella," said Olivia, her eyes shining. "I believe that's the most thrill I've had in my entire life. Shocking to be sure, and I'm so sorry about Gerard's involvement. It's not terribly unsurprising, I suppose. He has always been an ass, and it explains much about how he has foisted himself on you and your life. And the duke — oh, Isabella, he wants you, that much is certain."

Isabella nodded mutely, feeling quite drained all of a sudden as the excitement slid from her body and she was left with trepidation on what would happen to her next.

"For all that Bradley — the Duke of Carrington — has

shown interest in me, once all is public about Gerard, he will distance himself from me. I am not only the daughter of a disreputable viscount, but now my family is embroiled in further scandal against the entirety of the country."

"He knows you have done nothing to be at fault!" exclaimed Olivia.

"Thank you for your help, Olivia," Isabella said, ignoring her words with a small smile. "I trust you will not disclose this to anyone for the time being."

Olivia nodded. "Of course. And Isabella, please, stay away from Gerard, at least until the duke and Lord Kenley return. If you need anything, I am but a few doors away. Keep faith."

Isabella squeezed her hand in thanks as they climbed the stairs and said goodnight.

Once back in her bedchamber, with the doors firmly locked and with chairs placed in front of them, just to be doubly sure Gerard could not enter and surprise her, Isabella laid out each letter on the floor in front of her. She was grieved over what her stepbrother had chosen to do but knew that Gerard had always sought power. It appeared that he had managed to secure such a thing by involving himself in espionage. More than likely, it paid a pretty penny too – and Gerard had always been desperate to accumulate more and more wealth.

With a sinking heart, she began to read through the letters one at a time, seeing her stepbrother's developing involvement. Initially, he had started off by finding a few names for this man, Vaquelin, but had done more and more until he was sending back information on a regular basis.

There were requests for the names of those closest to the royal family, of those who had the highest titles and the greatest wealth. Vaquelin asked for information about the army, which, apparently, Gerard had struggled to supply. And then had come the warning that the Foreign Office was becoming a little more on their guard, and, however they had discovered it, there were men within society working for the Foreign Office.

There was no clear evidence showing how Gerard had known that Bradley and his friend Roger were the ones he was looking for, but she suspected that Bradley would pry that information from Gerard once he had been arrested.

Her heart had wrenched as she'd read Vaquelin's letter congratulating Gerard on successfully disposing of one man, but simultaneously warning him to find and dispatch the other as well. So this was what the duke's suspicions about the horse and the brandy had been regarding.

There was no question about it. Gerard was the man Bradley was looking for. He was the traitor. He was the conspirator. He was the murderer.

Slightly nauseous now, Isabella collected up all the letters, keeping the ones that revealed the most about Gerard's wrongdoings at the front of the pile. She was not quite sure what to do with them at first, knowing that she needed a good hiding place just in case Gerard came looking for them here should he realize they were gone. Whatever Lord Belrose had done, he was now on the run and she could not say what Gerard's reaction might be to that.

Opening the door to the small dressing room, she stepped inside and looked around the dusty room. Finding a small hiding place at the back of the large wardrobe in the corner, she placed the letters there carefully, before closing the dressing room door and locking it once more. Then, exhaustion filling her now, she removed her dress and slipped into her night things. Dawn was already breaking, but Isabella knew she would not be able to keep her eyes open for much longer, despite the thoughts whirling through her mind.

Lying down on her bed, she pulled the covers up to her chin and stared up at the ceiling. Life was about to change from this day onwards. Once Bradley had captured Gerard, there would be no need for Bradley to be in her life any longer.

Would he be anyway?

No. Isabella knew with certainty that he would never want to be with her after this, knowing what he did about her stepbrother. He may have been attracted to her, as he said, but she supposed all along, as she had heard him say to Lord Kenley, he had grown close to her to find out what he could about Gerard. He may have wanted her, but it was never anything permanent, especially now that he knew her stepbrother had been responsible for the death of his closest friend.

The treasure chest and its heirlooms no longer seemed to matter quite as much. Instead, replacing her urge to find the box and make her escape, she found that her longing was to be in the duke's arms, wishing that he was the one to give her the freedom she had been searching for.

## CHAPTER 18

Bradley spurred his horse to a gallop, with Alastair riding full out beside him. The grass was frosty under the horse's hooves, and he certainly had to ride with care in the dawning light, but his determination to catch Belrose encouraged him on. There had been a delay as they'd saddled their horses, finding no groomsmen about — which had not been surprising given the hour — but that delay had cost many precious minutes. He did not want Belrose to reach London, for then he could easily lose the man. He had no particular knowledge of where Belrose lived, nor who his friends and acquaintances were. The man could disappear and Bradley might never find him again for, by the time he found out the man's address from Isabella, Charles Belrose could have easily left the country.

His breath came in short gasps as he pushed his horse harder. Luckily, the mounts were fresh and keen to gallop, evidently enjoying the morning air. That, at least, was a blessing.

"Ho!" Alastair shouted, nodding to Bradley's left. "Look, there!"

To Bradley's very great relief, there was a carriage just turning around a slight bend in the road. It was not far and, within minutes, they had caught up with it.

"Stop there!" Bradley called, seeing the stunned expression on the coachman's face. "Stop there, I say!"

Charles Belrose's face appeared at the carriage window, looking more wraith than man. "Do not stop!" he screamed, thumping on the carriage roof for all he was worth. "Do not stop!"

Frustrated with Belrose's attempts to run from them, even though it was more than obvious that the game was up, Bradley pushed his horse just a little more and, together with Alastair, drew alongside the carriage horses. It did not take much for the horses to begin to slow, as the carriage driver was forced to tug at the reins in order to prevent an accident. Reaching out, Bradley caught the bridle of one of the horses and, despite the loud and vehement protests from Charles Belrose, managed to bring the carriage to a halt.

Throwing his reins to Alastair — who caught them deftly — Bradley slipped from his horse and made his way to the carriage, pulling the door open. Charles Belrose stared at him in horror, his skin milk white and eyes wide.

"Get out, Belrose," Bradley spat, his anger spiking. "This is all over."

"I haven't done anything," Belrose protested, scrambling back in his seat, away from Bradley. "I swear I have not. I am loyal to the Crown!"

"But Durand is not, and you knew about it," Bradley replied, firmly. "Get out now, Belrose. You are going to tell me everything you know or I shall hand you over to the executioner myself." He waited for a moment or two for the man to consider what he was saying, and, finally, Belrose made a move to shift forward out of his seat.

It took all of Bradley's patience not to reach in and grab

the man by the collar and drag him outside, gritting his teeth as Belrose descended from the carriage carefully.

"Speak," Bradley demanded, as Alastair came to join them. "What do you know of Gerard Durand?"

"He is a French spy," Belrose squeaked, his skin going a light shade of grey. "I had nothing to do with it, however. I simply became aware of what he was doing."

"And why did you not tell someone?" Alastair asked, his eyebrows furrowing. "You could have reported the man to the authorities."

Belrose did not reply, looking quite uncomfortable with the question. He dropped his head and stared at the ground as one foot twisted in the dirt.

"Ah," Bradley murmured, suddenly aware of why Belrose had not done such a thing, "because he offered you his sister's hand."

Belrose's head shot up.

"He threatened me," he said, with a flash of anger in his eyes. "The man is powerful. I could have been killed if I had said anything. There are more than just Durand in the country."

Bradley shook his head. "So you were looking out for yourself. And he sweetened his threats by telling you that you could wed Isabella, provided, of course, you give him half of her wealth in return."

His lip curled as he looked at Belrose, seeing him for the weak man he was. "You have been so easily caught up in that man's lies and falsehoods, Belrose," he continued, disdain filling him. "You should have stood up to him."

"You should have stood up for your country," Alastair added, firmly. "You have brought shame to yourself."

Belrose said nothing, his head drooping even further.

"Do you know anything of Gerard Durand's communication with a man called Vaquelin?" Bradley asked, recalling how he had overheard Durand talking with Belrose that day he had been forced to hide in the cabinet.

"No," Belrose replied, looking up at Bradley with desperation in his eyes. "I swear it. I did nothing to involve myself."

"Durand would not have included you whether you wished it or not, is that not so?" Bradley queried, seeing the defeat in the man's eyes. "He did not think you reliable. No, do not argue," he continued, seeing Belrose open his mouth to protest. "I overheard a conversation between the two of you. I am quite aware of the man's estimation of you."

There was a short pause. Belrose said nothing as Alastair and Bradley exchanged glances.

"Why did you run, Belrose?" Alastair asked, taking one step closer to the man. His voice became low and threatening as Belrose stood silently, refusing to answer.

"Speak to me, man, or it will be all the worse for you."

"Why? What is going to happen to me?" Belrose quavered, betraying the weakness that had gotten him into this situation in the first place. "Am I to face the noose?" His eyes roved from Alastair to Bradley and back again, terror evident on his face.

"Why did you run, Belrose?" Bradley repeated, refusing to answer the man's question. "Did you speak to Durand before you left?"

Belrose sighed heavily and shook his head. "I did not tell him I was going, but he will notice my absence and will suspect it is because of you."

"He knows who I am, then?"

Nodding, Belrose lifted one shoulder. "You are not surprised by this revelation, however. You knew he was trying to do away with you."

"I did."

Belrose nodded at Bradley's words. "Then the reasons for my absence will be clear to him. He will know that I thought you were getting a little too close for comfort and left."

"You must have heard us," Alastair said, quietly, "or seen us, this evening."

There was no use in Belrose denying it. "I did. I was not able to sleep and when I saw you walking down the stairs by candlelight to the study, I realized you had closed in on Durand and I thought it best I leave before anyone discovered my involvement."

"And yet, discovered you are, and your name will be provided to the powers-that-be," Bradley said, quietly.

"But I have told you everything!" Belrose exclaimed, horror-struck. "Please, I am not a traitor. I would not betray the Crown!" One of his hands went to his neck, as though he could already feel the hangman's noose. "I beg you to have mercy."

Bradley shook his head, stepped forward and indicated that Belrose should enter into the carriage once more. "That is not for me to decide, Belrose," he said, as the man climbed back inside. "That will be a matter for the Foreign Office. Now, get in. We have no time to waste."

Once Belrose was inside, Bradley turned to Alastair. "You must go with him, Kenley," he directed. "I shall have to ride on more quickly than the carriage can travel. Thank goodness London is not too far from here."

"You are worried about Miss Marriott."

Bradley nodded, unable to shake the feeling that she was in danger. "Once Durand realizes that we are gone, as well as Belrose, then his suspicions are bound to spike. I must fetch officials from the Foreign Office and return to her as soon as I can."

Alastair agreed, his expression serious. "I am sure she will have hidden the letters, Carrington, but you are quite right to be concerned. Durand is more dangerous than I first realized. Be on your guard."

Slapping Alastair on the back, Bradley shook his hand firmly and made his way over to his horse. Alastair would ensure that Charles Belrose was held firmly at the Foreign Office until Bradley returned, hopefully with Gerard Durand in tow.

All he could see was Isabella as he began to ride toward London. She had been courageous thus far, risking everything to help him, even though the consequences of her stepbrother's actions could reach far and wide. She could, simply through her relationship to Durand, become shunned by all of society, though he was not quite certain that she would find this a particular trial.

She was seeking freedom, to live as she wished and, he was quite sure, to live quietly. After all that had gone on, the solace of living without her stepbrother beside her was sure to be more healing than anything.

Bradley also realized that once he had Durand arrested, there would be no particular reason for him to remain by her side, at her home, but his heart simply refused to allow that idea to take hold. He did not want to lose her.

Would she consider marriage to him?

When Bradley thought about a potential wife, he couldn't see anyone *but* Isabella. She may not be of a status that would typically be considered acceptable, but he found he no longer overly cared.

He had initially convinced himself he felt nothing for her. Then he had admitted he desired her more than he ever had another. And now… now he didn't see how he could ever be without her. To return to London and his life before Isabella filled him with dread instead of eagerness.

She had returned his kisses with a passion that had both

surprised him and heated his blood. Could she hold any affection in return, despite all that they had been through?

Tonight she had helped him, trusted him, believed in him, and done everything she could to support him in his quest. Even still, she was waiting for his return, despite what that might mean for her.

*I love her.*

The realization sent shockwaves through him. He had never considered himself in love before and had not even been open to it, but now, with only a few weeks acquaintance, his depth of emotion for Isabella Marriott overwhelmed him. She was in his every thought, his every consideration. Her smile made his heart sing, her touch made his body soar.

Her dark hair and warm brown eyes captivated him, her pert lips and supple curves caught him. He couldn't go back to how things were. He could only go forward.

"I shall have to tell her how I feel," he said aloud, both gleeful and nervous in equal measure, "after this whole sordid business is settled."

Even his horse seemed to agree with his sentiments, for it tossed its head and snorted, making Bradley chuckle. He had every hope that she would accept him and that, together, they could start a new life, free from the sins of Gerard Durand.

## CHAPTER 19

"Isabella!"

Befuddled, Isabella sat up on her bed, rubbing one hand across her eyes. There was a loud hammering on her door and her name was being called repeatedly.

"Isabella! Open up at once!"

Groaning, she looked at the still-drawn curtains, seeing the beams of light shine through. She had very little idea of how long she had been asleep for, but evidently Gerard had discovered the absence of some of his guests, and possibly his papers. A shiver ran across her skin as she thought about last night's events. If Bradley was not back yet — and it seemed too early for him to have returned — she was entirely at her stepbrother's mercy. Thankfully there was no reason for him to suspect her of anything untoward.

The pounding on the door became more insistent, her stepbrother's voice growing even louder. Isabella knew she could no longer pretend to still be asleep, for his knocking was loud enough to wake the dead. Reminding herself to deny all knowledge of what had taken place, Isabella stumbled from her bed and opened the door, wearing her planned pained expression.

"Gerard? Whatever is the matter?"

"Still abed, sister?" he sneered, one lip curling. "Or is there someone there with you?"

A frisson of fear raced through her chest. "Do not be so ridiculous, Gerard. I did not sleep well last night and my headache has returned. Please leave. I must return to my bed."

She tried to shut the door on him, but it was of no use.

"I do not think so."

He shoved the door, hard, and she was forced to step back to let him in. She frowned as he stood, his hands firmly on his hips as he surveyed the room. Isabella maintained calm, not wanting to anger him further, even though his actions were quite intrusive. She had been handling Gerard for long enough now. There was no reason she couldn't do so today.

"Gerard," she said, placatingly. "Whatever are you doing? Can you not see that I am still in my night things? I must return to bed. My head is quite painful and the light is hurting."

"The duke is not with you, then?"

Isabella gasped, feigning indignance, although the truth was, she more than wished that he was with her. "How dare you suggest such a thing? No, indeed he is not! Do you wish to search for him?"

Gerard sneered mockingly. "Don't think that I have been unaware of his attentions toward you, Isabella. His room is next to yours, after all. Have you hidden him in that small dressing room, which you've been using for liaisons?"

Isabella shook her head. "Gerard, you are being ridiculous."

She waited with her heart in her mouth as he moved to the small room, turning the handle but finding it locked. As she had hidden the letters there, she tried not to allow her anxiety show on her face, and when he demanded that she find the key to open it, she had no choice but to do so without question.

Once the door was unlocked, Gerard stormed inside while she remained in her room, her arms crossed over herself as though they would protect her. The letters were well hidden, and she did not *think* that Gerard would find them, but she couldn't be certain. After a few minutes, her stepbrother returned with a furious expression. His lips were almost white with rage, his eyes narrowed.

"The duke is not in his room," he breathed, fury in every word.

Isabella tried to look surprised, as well as entirely innocent of any knowledge of where the duke was, though relief flooded through her knowing that Bradley and Lord Kenley had managed to escape without notice.

"Tell me where he's gone, Isabella."

"Gone?" she repeated, "I know nothing about where he is gone. I would have thought him within his chamber."

She thought she had convinced him. But then he stepped forward and slapped her full across the face with the back of his hand. Stunned by the pain now throbbing through her head, she stumbled back, pressing one hand to her cheek. Blinking through the stars that spun around her head, she tried to keep her composure.

"You will not strike me again, Gerard," she said, firmly, refusing to be intimidated. "Do not raise a hand to me – ever again – or it will be all the worse for you."

He laughed scornfully, his lips thinning as he surveyed her. "You have always been too stubborn, Isabella, although I must say that I find your threats quite laughable." He shook his head and began to advance toward her, and Isabella could not help but panic. "I'm going to ask you again, Isabella. Where has the duke gone to? Where is his friend?"

"I do not know, Gerard," she repeated, in as firm a voice as she could manage. Unfortunately, the door to her bedchamber was just behind Gerard and Isabella did not think she could escape past him. Why had she not run out when he had gone to the dressing room?

Because she had underestimated him.

Frustrated with herself for not thinking of it before now, she tried to keep her voice light. "I did not know that he was not in his room, Gerard. As you saw, I keep the door to the adjoining dressing room locked and I have been in bed with a headache since last evening. He has left the estate, you say?"

"Yes, I believe he has," Gerard grated, his eyes narrowing. "As has his friend, Lord Kenley and even Lord Belrose!"

"Lord Belrose?" Isabella repeated in a puzzled voice. "I had not thought them a friendly pair. Why should they leave together? And what is it about their disappearance that concerns you so? Perhaps they have simply gone for an early-morning jaunt."

There was a long pause and Isabella held her breath, aware of just how carefully Gerard was studying her.

"You are not a particularly good liar, Isabella. The reason that I am so concerned is that my study door was unlocked this morning, even though I am the only one who has a key to that particular room."

Isabella tried to laugh, although it came out as a croak. "You cannot think that I somehow broke into your study to steal documents, Gerard. I have no idea how to pick a lock, and I certainly could not get the key, given that you kept the only copy."

She saw Gerard give her a wolfish smile and, with dawning horror, realized what, through her nervousness, she had inadvertently revealed. Fear raced through her veins, turning her to ice. She was now clearly in Gerard's sights, the bird in range of the bullet. His eyes were trained on her, a stealth in his stance that had her shrinking inwardly.

"Now, sister dear," he said, quietly, moving closer despite her efforts to back away. "How did you know that some of my documents have been taken if you were, as you say, tossing and turning in your bed all evening?"

"I – " her mouth went dry as she saw the fury in his eyes, her back now pressed against the wall by the fireplace. Her hands scrabbled for something she could use to defend herself, and she found the cold metal of the fire poker behind her.

"He took them, didn't he?" Gerard growled, a murderous look in his eyes. "And you saw your opportunity to get rid of me, did you?" He lunged at her, but Isabella brought the poker up at once, knocking his arm away from her.

"You will not touch me, Gerard."

"You will not be able to stop me," he growled, his face red with anger. "You have no one to defend you."

"Carrington is returning," she replied, still holding the poker toward him despite its heaviness.

He sneered. "By the time Carrington gets back to this estate, you and I will be long gone. A brothel in Paris for you, I think."

She shuddered, grasping the poker with both hands as she slowly moved to the door. She was determined to escape this situation, quite sure that her stepbrother meant every word he said. "Carrington will find me, Gerard," she said, softly. "He cares for me."

Gerard laughed and reached out for her again, but Isabella struck out and hit him across the forearm, forcing him to back away.

"He will never find you in the depths of the Paris slums," he snarled, his eyes darkening with fury. "You must realize the man doesn't care for you, Isabella. You were a pawn, a means to an end. He had a little fun with you on the way, but he's gone now that he has what he wants. Give it up now, Isabella. You will never be able to defend yourself alone."

"She is not alone."

The words came through the door as it flew open and Isabella almost collapsed with relief at the sight of Bradley standing there with a group of men behind him. She dropped the poker, which landed with a clatter, and backed away from Gerard.

"Any threats made to my betrothed are threats made to me, Durand," she heard Bradley say, and she lifted her head in disbelief. "You have already killed my best friend. I will not allow you to take any more lives – especially not hers." There was a pause as he crossed to her, tightening an arm around her waist. "Your time as a free man is over," he finished, as two of the men came in to lead Gerard away.

Isabella stood gaping, and she noticed the hallway had filled with their houseguests. Whatever they had thought they knew before, they all were more than aware now.

* * *

ISABELLA SAT QUIETLY in her bedchamber, waiting patiently for the duke to return once more. The Foreign Office had taken Gerard away and she had carefully retrieved the letters and handed them over to Bradley, who had placed them in a small box. Two of the riders were now on their way to London with the letters in their possession. The duke and the Foreign Office were taking no chances.

Some of the men from the Foreign Office remained. Isabella had disbanded the house party with the smallest amount of scandal possible. She had thanked each of the guests for coming and declared that a family matter had caused her to discontinue the festivities.

Of course, they had all been eager for more details, but Isabella had been firm. Only Olivia knew the full story, and before she left with her parents she had given Isabella's arm a squeeze, as she told her to stay strong and send for her if any help was needed. Isabella nodded, grateful for her and the fact that, in the end, Olivia had proven more than trustworthy.

Now, Isabella sat alone in the silence of the house, unsure of what to think.

Reflecting on all that had happened, Isabella swung her foot idly as she sat by the fireplace and looked into the flames. Life was going to be very different now, but just how different remained to be seen.

Life without Bradley, or life with him.

When he had announced her as his betrothed in front of Gerard, her heart had blossomed with happiness, as she was thrilled at the thought of being with him for the rest of her life. But then again, he had not actually proposed to her, and she was worried that he had only said such a thing in front of Gerard to prove that she was under his protection.

Did he actually want to wed her? Their relationship was not one of long acquaintance, but they had gone through so much together in that short time that she felt as though she knew him very well indeed. He was kind and considerate, thoughtful and witty, and, while he had not always told her the whole truth about his plans and intentions, she knew he had never hidden those things from her in order to deceive her. He had proven his strength of character over and over again, and now Isabella could not think of being without him.

To go back to a life alone seemed empty and dreary, her heart growing sick at the thought. Yes, she would have the freedom she had longed for, but it would not be a happy life if Bradley were not a part of it. Her drive to find the box no longer had the same sense of urgency, for, even though she wanted to find her family heirloom, Isabella knew that she did not need it in order to live contentedly.

If her experience with Gerard had taught her anything, it was that a great deal of wealth didn't make for a happy life. But did Bradley truly want her, or now that this was all over would he return home, back to his previous life, where he would find himself a beautiful, titled duchess among the many women who vied for his affections?

She just couldn't be sure.

The thought nearly broke her.

CHAPTER 20

"Ah, my dear Isabella."
The door to her bedchamber opened and Bradley stepped inside, his face wreathed in smiles. She rose at once, trepidation on her face, but he caught her hands, looking down at her with tenderness.

"Is it all over?" she asked, her heart fluttering in her chest at the look in his eyes.

"Yes, it is," he replied softly, brushing one finger down her cheek. "The remainder of the house guests have left, though I am sorry to say that I will not be able to prevent their gossiping tongues from setting London ablaze with all that has happened here."

"That is just what I expected," Isabella replied, her skin burning from where he had touched her. "And certainly not your fault. I cannot thank you enough for all you have done."

He smiled, although his eyes held concern. "Are you sure you are all right, Isabella? I know you disliked him, but he was your stepbrother after all."

Appreciating his consideration for her, Isabella smiled up at him. "Truthfully, I am quite well. Yes, he was my stepbrother, but not for much time. He is a traitor to the Crown and a murderer, and I am glad to be rid of that connection."

She did not want to ask what would happen to Gerard, knowing quite well what the punishment was for treason. "I am just sorry that he killed your friend, Bradley."

Swaying slightly, she caught his arm for support, suddenly thinking of what Gerard had tried to do to the duke. The horse ride and the brandy could easily have brought about his death. She was just glad that he had his wits about him and had not drunk the poisoned brandy.

"Then, if you are quite well, I think we should talk about the future," he said, quietly, putting his hands on her waist to steady her. "I know that I referred to you as my betrothed in front of your stepbrother, and I will be honest – that felt quite right."

He looked down at her, his face serious, and Isabella's heart lifted, but she didn't want to allow her hope to rise with it.

"It feels as though you should be with me, Isabella, that we should share our lives together. There is a bond between us now that just doesn't seem right to break."

Isabella let out a long breath, her stomach swirling with varying emotions. "Are you sure that is what you truly want? I don't want you to feel obligated. So much has happened that I am now wrapped up in disrepute of the present as well as the past. I am a scandalized viscount's daughter and a traitor's stepsister. You have your choice of women, Bradley. You are a duke. And I —"

He stopped her flow of words with a searing kiss.

"I want no other, Isabella. Only you. I don't care about what your father did, or what your stepbrother did. None of that was your fault. All I care is that you will be by my side. The only question is – do you want me as well?"

"I do, Bradley," she said, laughing with tears in her eyes.

His face lit up with delight, his hands tightening around her waist. "Then, would you do me the honor of becoming my wife, Isabella? I will give you all the freedom you wish and swear that I shall never, ever, dictate your life for you. Our lives shall be a joining, a partnership, intertwined together with love and affection."

His voice grew a little hoarse as he rested his forehead against hers, his breath whispering across her cheek. "I do believe that I am in love with you, Isabella. So, tell me… what do you say?"

Isabella closed her eyes, wanting to savor every moment. Her arms wrapped around his neck, her heart filled with love for him. "Nothing would make me happier," she breathed, overcome. "I love you with my whole heart, Bradley. I cannot imagine being without you."

He kissed her almost as soon as she finished speaking, her words caught by his lips. He was hungry for her. She could feel it in the urgency of his kiss, in the fire that scorched through her. Isabella framed his face with her hands and kissed him back, pressing the length of her body against his. Breaking the kiss for a moment, she heard a small groan emerge from him, before he caught her around the waist and lifted her to her tiptoes.

When he finally released her, she stumbled back a little, only for him to reach out for her again. Her shoulder glanced off the mantlepiece as he caught her, but in her happiness, she hardly even felt it.

"Wait!"

Bradley set her down slowly, his eyes not on her anymore, but beyond her, on the ground. She stared up at him, puzzled at what could be so much more interesting.

"What is it?" she asked, following his gaze – and there, on the floor, lay a small brown book with a diamond in the center. Her heart slammed into her chest, her breath catching as, with trembling fingers, she bent to pick it up.

"Is that…?"

She nodded, tracing one finger down the small book. "Yes, this is what I have been searching for." She looked up at him, bewildered. "Where did it come from?"

Bradley frowned and moved to the mantlepiece. "I believe it came from the mantlepiece somewhere. You knocked against it and the next thing I saw, the book was on the floor."

Isabella could hardly believe what she was holding, as memories of her grandmother flooded through her. Together, they looked at the mantlepiece, unable to see where the book had come from – until Bradley spotted something.

"Look, here," he exclaimed, crouching on his knees and pointing to a long, thin recess cut into the left side of the mantlepiece. "It must have been in here."

Staring at it, Isabella could not help but laugh, shaking her head to herself. "How like my grandmother! She put it somewhere my father wouldn't find it, knowing that he would never think to look somewhere like this in here."

Looking around her room, her expression softened. "This has always been my room. My grandmother must have had this placed in here somehow, knowing that I would not rest until I found the box. I searched this room multiple times, but had never thought to look here."

Bradley rose and smiled at her, his expression soft. "I am very glad for you, love. Family heirlooms deserve to be treasured, kept safe with you instead of buried in the earth."

Isabella smiled back at him. "Yes, I believe they do. This diary will tell me all that I need to know."

"Just so long as you are not planning to escape to the Americas once you find the jewelry box," he replied, with a twinkle of laughter in his eye. "I am quite determined to keep you here, Isabella."

Laughing now, she shook her head. "No, I confess that the Americas do not hold the same enticement they once did." Her gaze grew a little coy as he tugged her closer to him. "Although, if I did, would you come after me?"

"Without a moment's hesitation," he replied, his voice low and filled with warmth. "I would chase you around the world, if I had to, Isabella."

If she smiled any wider, her lips might crack. "I could not be without you either, Bradley. I seem to have found the diary at the perfect time."

He caught her against him once more, the diary falling to the floor. His mouth was fire itself, burning her to the very core. Isabella gave herself up to him at once, suddenly desperate for her fiancé to satisfy the longing that he had sparked the moment he entered this house. She hesitatingly whispered as such to him.

"Now?" he asked, stepping back as his eyes searched her face.

She took advantage of the pause to find his waistcoat and begin to unbutton it. "We can be married in no time at all."

She nodded fiercely. "I am sure, and I do not want to wait any longer. I want to be with you, *now*, on this day of new beginnings. Show me how much you love me, Bradley – please?"

Bradley did not wait, catching her around the waist and lifting her up bodily, before depositing her on the bed. His eyes flickered over her before he began to slowly and methodically undress before her. Isabella watched him hungrily, unsure what exactly it was she was eager for but breathlessly awaiting it nonetheless.

His bare skin was all she could look at, her tongue tracing her dry lips. The pace of her heart picked up with each item of clothing discarded, and she gasped in surprise as he revealed himself to her in his entirety.

"Don't be afraid," he murmured, drawing closer to her and beginning to pluck the pins from her hair, until it fell from its binds and flowed in glossy black waves around her shoulders. "We are to be man and wife and will often be as naked as the day we were born."

"Often?" Isabella squeaked out, finding it difficult just to draw breath.

He chuckled. "Yes, very often, if I have my way." He leaned over and kissed her slowly, until she was lying flat on the bed, his body over hers.

"And if I don't want to sometimes?" she asked, although if this was any indication of what was in store, she couldn't see herself ever resisting.

"Then we won't," he responded.

"You will not… go to another? I know men are wont to do so."

"Never," he said with vehemence. "You are the only one for me now."

She was on fire at once, every part of her slowly building to a burn. Bradley broke the kiss and brushed her hair from her face, a small smile on his lips.

"You are beautiful, Isabella, both inside and out. I love you with every part of me and will show you just how much."

She could not speak, her breath coming out in a ragged gasp as he suddenly tugged the shoulders of her dress down, revealing her nakedness to him. To her surprise, she had no urge to cover up, but only a longing to have his skin against hers.

"We shall have to undress you, my love," he whispered, suddenly pulling back and grasping her hands. Isabella rose on unsteady legs and, within minutes, everything was discarded on the floor. Her blood thickened as he laid her back down, her body beginning to cry out for his touch once more.

Isabella closed her eyes as he kissed her slowly, taking his time with her and letting her become used to his caresses. His hands moved to her breasts, his fingers gently running over them – and Isabella almost came off the bed with his touch.

"This is only the beginning, Isabella," he murmured, evidently delighted at her response to him. His head lowered to where his hands had been, his mouth dragging over her breasts, as he tenderly loved each of them, one after the other. She raised her head from the pillow as his hands moved lower, and she was suddenly all too aware of the pooling heat in the very center of her.

"Trust me, Isabella," he breathed, his fingers brushing against her nub ever so slightly. Isabella was astonished at the moan that escaped from her lips, her eyes closing again of their own accord. The pleasurable ache between her legs grew with intensity, making her shudder.

Bradley kissed her neck once more as his fingers roved over her thighs near the place where pressure was building. Isabella felt entirely exposed to him, open completely, but reveled in the sensation. Managing to open her eyes, she saw him gaze up at her with adoration, the heat of his own passion evident in the icy blue depths of his eyes.

"You must not be afraid to let go," he said, making her frown in confusion. "And there will be some pain, but only for a moment."

"I trust you, Bradley," she managed to whisper, her eyes closing again as he began to kiss a trail down toward her breasts once more.

Breathing hard, Isabella arched against Bradley as his mouth caught her nipple, his fingers rubbing gently at the place where it seemed like every piece of her was centered.

She was growing closer to something, something that she was afraid would shatter her completely as she scrabbled at his shoulders, her fingers digging into his skin.

An explosion of pleasure rushed down upon her, causing her entire body to tense before she began to twist beneath him, unable to breathe, unable to think. Her body pulsed of its own accord, shattering her completely. And there, through it all, was Bradley whispering her name, giving her words of love, telling her to trust him.

When the sensation passed, Isabella felt something press against her, and she opened her eyes to see Bradley atop her, his blue eyes crystal and filled with heat. He looked as though he was holding himself back from something, something that took a great deal of strength.

"Remember," he grunted, his mouth inches from hers, "pain for a moment, but soon, pleasure. Last chance — are you sure, darling?"

She did not know what to think, but nodded, giving him her trust. When he slowly filled her with his hard length, she felt a twist deep within her, making her cry out. He stilled at once, his eyes looking at her with concern, as he waited for her throbbing ache to pass.

Eventually it did so, and with it came a myriad of sensations. Isabella realized that she was, now, truly joined to this man and, as he began to move within her again, found that the pain was slowly being replaced with pleasure.

His steady driving thrusts, gentle at first, but slowly increasing in momentum, had her gasping for breath, her body beginning to spike with pleasure once more. His mouth found hers, and his tongue moved in time with the rest of his body. When he moved faster, she had no choice but to arch her back, cries issuing from her throat as her body tensed once again. It was as though she were carried on the crest of a wave, just waiting for it to crash her back down.

As his body went taut, her core filled with a sudden, unexpected warmth. His mouth tore at hers, and Isabella soared again, stars sparkling in her vision. Their kiss broke, both of them taking in ragged breaths as he touched his forehead to hers.

"So," he whispered, a laughing smile on his face, "what say you, my dear Isabella? Once we are wed, shall you be in my bed very often do you think?"

Isabella smiled, her mind and heart filled only with her duke. "Yes, I think so. Very often, indeed."

He chuckled. "I am glad to hear it. For I intend to spend the rest of my life showing you how much I love ever part of you – your kindness, your patience, your strength."

Reaching up, she caressed his silky locks, overcome with all that had occurred and where she currently found herself.

"There will never be another in my heart," she promised. "I love you, Bradley, more than I can ever say."

# EPILOGUE

"Ah, so it falls to me to do the digging!"

Isabella laughed and leaned forward to kiss him on the cheek. "If you do this for me, then I promise you that I will find some way to reward you." Her cheeks burned at the suggestive words, smiling when he grinned at her, his eyes turning the icy blue as they always did when he especially desired her.

They had married by special license soon after the house party. While they made their home at Bradley's estate and the London manor, of course, they kept Isabella's home as well. She reflected on all that had happened, how her future had changed so drastically in such a short time.

"I have always said that you are too tempting for words," he said with a wink before his mouth landed on hers, his strong hand pulling her to him, but Isabella pushed away, laughing.

"Digging first," she protested, seeing him grin, "kissing later."

He muttered something under his breath but began to dig, great clods of mud flying up into the air. Isabella

ONCE UPON A DUKE'S DREAM

shrieked with laughter and moved out of the way, excitement growing in her chest.

The diary had given very clear instructions as to where the heirlooms could be found and it had not been Isabella's eagerness that had driven them here, but rather Bradley's. She had been worried that he would think she might want to make her escape if she seemed too keen to find it, but had soon lost that particular concern.

He was as assured of her love as she was of his, with no doubt in his mind over their future. And so, having followed the directions carefully, they had found themselves in front of a beautiful rose bush, the scent reminding Isabella of her grandmother.

"She loved roses," she sighed to herself, as Bradley continued to dig. How like her grandmother to place the box in a spot where Isabella would be reminded of her.

"Here we go," Bradley grunted as his shovel struck something hard, and he wiped his forehead with the back of his hand.

"Careful!" Isabella exclaimed as he continued to dig, albeit with a little more care. Putting her hands by her mouth, she tried to wait patiently, even though her nerves jangled with every dig of his shovel.

Eventually, Bradley leaned down into the hole he'd dug and slowly, with great care, lifted a heavy box to the surface. Isabella gasped, her eyes filling with sudden tears as she knelt down on the damp grass, her fingers running over the surface of the roughly hewn box.

"That's it?"

Bradley threw himself down next to her, his breath coming in short, sharp gasps as he recovered from his exertions.

Isabella laughed softly, wiping the tears from her cheek. "She put it in this box to keep it safe," she explained, her fingers brushing the old, worn catch at the front. "Here, look." She lifted the catch, pulled back the lid and gasped in astonishment at the treasure that lay before her.

There sat the ruby-encrusted box, its vibrancy catching the sunlight. With trembling hands, she lifted the lid of that box and found inside the precious family heirloom. She let her fingers touch the cool surface of the gems, her mind filled with memories of her grandmother.

"Well, you certainly would have had enough to pay your way to the Americas," Bradley murmured, moving to sit behind her, putting one hand around her waist as she leaned back against him. "What a considerate woman your grandmother must have been."

"She was," Isabella replied, quietly. "But now I have no need to sell it. I shall wear it often and think of her every time it is placed around my neck."

She looked up at him and saw him smile as his lips brushed her forehead.

"You are the greatest treasure I could ever have found," he murmured, softly. "More precious than rubies and worth more than gold."

They were more than words. Bradley had told her that while he could never right the past and bring Roger back, he had found his justice. He no longer woke up with nightmares – at least not often. And when he did, as soon as he realized Isabella was with him, they fled.

Isabella sighed happily, her future as bright as the sparkling diamonds in her hand. She would never again be terrified for her future, pressed under the rule of her stepbrother. That part of her life was over for good.

She was in the only place she now cared to be.

In the arms of her duke.

* * *

**THE END**

\* \* \*

Dear reader,

I hope you enjoyed reading Bradley and Isabella's story! If you had fun getting to know Olivia and Alastair, then you will love their story, which you can preview in the pages just after this one, or download here: He's a Duke, But I Love Him.

If you haven't yet signed up for my newsletter, I would love to have you join! You will receive Unmasking a Duke for free, as well as links to giveaways, sales, new releases, and stories about my coffee addiction, my struggle to keep my plants alive, and how much trouble one loveable wolf-lookalike dog can get into.

www.elliestclair.com/ellies-newsletter

You will also receive links to giveaways, sales, updates, launch information, promos, and the newest recommended reads.

Or you can join my Facebook group, Ellie St. Clair's Ever Afters, and stay in touch daily.

Happy reading!

With love,
Ellie

\* \* \*

## He's a Duke, But I Love Him
## Happily Ever After Book 4

After five seasons, Lady Olivia Jackson has despaired of ever finding the man she is searching for -- a man who will allow her the freedom to live life as she pleases. Her deepest desires are not the typical pastimes of a lady. Using a pseudonym, Olivia puts her intellect to use writing a financial column, and yearns for a life of fun and adventure. Her mother, unfortunately, has other ideas.

Upon the unexpected death of his father, well-known rake and charmer Alastair Finchley is thrust into the role of Duke of Breckenridge. The title, however, also comes with massive amounts of debt which his father accumulated at the horse track and the gambling tables. This life of responsibility is not one which Alastair would have chosen, and he is determined to maintain his rakish ways in all other aspects.

When Olivia and Alastair renew their acquaintance, they are shocked by the depths of their desire for one another. They each determine, however, that giving in is not worth the potential consequences -- or is it?

\* \* \*

# AN EXCERPT FROM HE'S A DUKE, BUT I LOVE HIM

*Oh*, blast.

Lady Olivia Jackson just barely kept the expletive from crossing her lips as she took in her mother, Lady Sutcliffe, grasping the large envelope between her long bony fingers.

"Mother," Olivia said with a nod as she entered the opulent drawing room, its rose walls, gilded ormolu Wedgwood chandelier and intricate roses carved and painted throughout portraying her mother's touch. Lady Sutcliffe adored redecorating, and had transformed the London manor into a garish, elaborate little girl's dollhouse brought to life. It suffocated Olivia, but any time she voiced her opinion to her mother, she was met with a harsh stare down her nose and a sniff, telling Olivia all she needed to know.

"Olivia," her mother said in greeting, while Olivia's sister, Helen, smiled at her from the settee in the corner of the room. Olivia had hardly noticed her, so quiet she was with her nose buried deep in the book in front of her.

"I just received the strangest correspondence," Lady Sutcliffe continued. "In actual fact, I did not receive it myself;

however it was delivered to our door. Jenkins was quite insistent that no one by this name lived here, but the delivery boy was not deterred. Have you ever heard the name P.J. Scott?"

Despite the fact she had never been one to hide a secret well, Olivia attempted to keep her expression light as she pushed down the alarm that rose from within.

"Ah, yes, actually, silly me," she said with a tinkling laugh that sounded forced even to her own ears. "It is a name I have been using for … correspondence."

Her mother raised her rather pointed eyebrows as her gaze focused on her eldest daughter.

"Correspondence with whom?"

"That is the point of the assumed name, Mother," said Olivia, "To keep the correspondence hidden."

"I am your mother, Olivia," Lady Sutcliffe responded. "You need not keep such secrets from me."

As her mother made to open the envelope, Olivia stepped forward, rather desperate as she panicked to determine how to stop her. She said the only thing she knew would keep her mother from opening the envelope and thus revealing its contents.

"It is simply a silly love note from a suitor, and he would wish to keep his thoughts for me alone," she said in a rush. "I'm sure he would be quite embarrassed should my mother read his words. Not that he writes anything that would be considered inappropriate, it is simply —"

"A suitor?" A smile crossed the usually tight, drawn face, and Olivia knew she had said the right thing. She had distracted her mother with enough information to keep her thoughts occupied. "I am thrilled, Olivia. Who is this mysterious man?"

"Umm it's … that is …"

Growing impatient, her mother picked up her letter

opener from her small writing desk, intricately carved with the roses she so adored.

"Lord Kenley!" The name burst out from Olivia's lips. Where in heaven's name did that come from? She had met the man once at a house party. They had slightly flirted, to no great significance, and she had seen him but once since then, from across the room at her friend's wedding. He was, to Olivia's thinking, too handsome. He knew to what extent he attracted young women and he used it to his advantage.

Sadly, Olivia realized she had thought of him likely because so few other men had given her much notice in the past few months. True, she was never without a dance partner and found many men to be friendly with her, but none had any serious interest in her for anything other than a flirt at the many social events she attended. At one time she had been highly sought after, particularly due to her rather large dowry, but not only did she push away men with her propensity to say anything that entered her mind, but she had refused a rather high number of suitors and proposals, and the men simply had stopped asking.

"Lord Kenley?" her mother murmured. "Well now, that is quite the news. He is an earl, is he not? His father a duke?"

"I believe so," she said with a shrug, feigning nonchalance.

"Olivia." The force of her mother's brilliant blue gaze, similar to her own yet with such an icy steel to it, bore into her. "This is a *very* good match for you. You must not muddle this particular courtship."

"Oh Mother, I do not believe anything shall come of it at all," Olivia attempted to dissuade her mother, and to prevent her from taking any action regarding this ridiculous lie she had so quickly concocted out of desperation.

"Then you must ensure something does come of it, Olivia," she said with a sniff. "You have been out now one season too many for a respectable young woman. Any more and you should be considered a spinster, and then no one will ever want you. Now, do hurry, we are expected for tea at Lady Branwood's by four. Come and prepare yourself, Helen."

With that, she threw the envelope down on the table and stormed out of the room. With a sympathetic glance her way, Helen, younger than Olivia by four years, followed in her wake. Helen was a sweet soul, but well under the thumb of their domineering mother.

While Olivia's mother had always been concerned about her prospects, they had intensified of late, likely because of Helen. Her sister had now been out a season herself, her parents deciding they could no longer wait for Olivia to be married in order for Helen to begin her own search for a husband. Olivia knew her mother still hoped that she should find a suitable match first, however. It seemed to be becoming more and more unlikely, and Olivia knew her mother despaired of having two daughters left unmarried.

She shouldn't have chosen the lie she did, but she knew her mother would not have relented, and it would have been far worse had she opened the package.

Olivia sighed as she picked up the envelope as well as the letter opener from her mother's writing desk, and sliced through the seal.

This had turned into an utter disaster. She had known better than to have the correspondence delivered to the house. She had always been so diligent in picking up and dropping it off to the journal's office herself, but with an engagement the evening prior that left her sleeping well into late morning and the tea planned for this afternoon, she had no time in which to leave the house. She had thought she would intercept the post before her mother saw it, but she had been too late.

She was eager to read the envelope's contents, however,

and hurried out of the parlor to the library, her own sanctuary. It was the one room in the manor that her mother had left untouched, and the masculine tones of the walls lined with the floor-to-ceiling mahogany shelves filled with leather-bound volumes provided Olivia with a sense of comfort. She took to the brass inlaid library table her father had set aside for her use as a desk in the corner of the room, and dumped out the contents of the envelope on its surface.

She set aside the note from Mr. Ungar and began to look more eagerly through the first query on the page in front of her.

*"Dr. Mr. Scott,*

*I have been reading your column in The Financial Register and I find your thoughts quite provoking and extraordinary. I am looking for advice regarding a particular investment of mine. Some months ago it was doing particularly well, and following the actions of a friend I placed a large portion of my income in such investment. I have now found the investment to be performing rather poorly. What should my next course of action be?*

*Sincerely,*
*Your Faithful Reader*

Olivia sighed as she read through the words and sat down on her leather-upholstered chair. Why in heaven's name would someone invest so much money simply because an acquaintance had done so? Well, there was nothing she could say to this man to better his current finances, but perhaps with a few sage words of advice, she could help others.

She tipped her quill pen in the ink blotter, and was about

to begin her scrawl across the paper in answer to the question in front of her. She had read through the financial sections and journals over the past week, although this answer was simply plain common sense more than anything. She thought of the many people in the world who took such poor care of their finances, and she shook her head in frustration.

"Lady Olivia?"

Olivia cringed as she heard the voice of her lady's maid, Molly, at the door. Oh yes, the tea. She did look a bit of a fright, and had to change for the visit before their departure. The simple white muslin morning dress she currently wore would never do.

She would have to return to this later, she thought with a frown, and tucked the correspondence deep into her pockets before scurrying out of the room and up the stairs to finish her preparations, bemoaning the time these functions took away from the research and writing she truly enjoyed.

\* \* \*

She said as much under her breath to her friend, Lady Rosalind Kennedy, as they sipped their tea slightly away from the circle of women in Lady Branwood's parlor later that afternoon.

Rosalind was one of very few people who knew of Olivia's secret identity. She was Olivia's oldest, closest friend, and luckily they often found themselves at similar functions.

Oh, how much easier it would be if she could simply be truthful and attach her own name to her work! She knew, however, that would never happen. No journal would ever publish financial advice from a woman, and no man would ever read her words seriously. She must be grateful that she had, at the very least, the ability to continue writing her financial column, even if that meant under an assumed man's name.

She drew Rosalind away from the others to take a moment to fill her in on the latest developments.

"Are you sure this remains a good idea?" Rosalind asked her with some trepidation as they stood by the tall sash window overlooking the street below, away from the prying ears of their mothers and other ladies of their acquaintance.

Rosalind looked rather pretty that afternoon, her long light brown hair pulled back off her face and into a low chignon at the nape of her neck. She appreciated Olivia's work and admired her friend for not only her intelligence but her ambition; however, she would never have attempted anything such as this on her own.

"Perhaps you should leave this behind you for some time," said Rosalind, "and focus on other things."

"Other things," Olivia snorted. "I assume you mean finding a husband for myself? I have told you, Rosalind, I am not sure how I am supposed to find a man willing to marry me for more than my dowry, who I find sufferable in return."

"For a woman offering financial and investment advice to men across London and beyond, I believe you have the ability to solve the problem of finding yourself a decent husband," said Rosalind with a wry grin.

"I have tried," Olivia replied, jutting out her chin. "And I have not found who I am searching for. Perhaps such a man simply does not exist."

"Oh?" said Rosalind, raising an eyebrow. "And who exactly is it that you are searching so hard for, who you have not found in five years at the balls you have attended and parties that your mother has arranged?"

"Someone who will not care that his wife is a financial columnist, who will give me the utmost freedom to do whatever I choose, who will stay out of my affairs, and yet, is enjoyable to speak to day in and day out," said Olivia. "That is who I require."

"Hmm," Rosalind replied with a nod. "I can see your dilemma. Finding such a man could be quite impossible. You have high standards, Olivia."

"I do, indeed," she said, and smiled. "It's my father's fault, I suppose. If only I could find a man like him. One who is warm, friendly, who would love his children with all his heart, and who would allow his wife to chase her heart's desire, whatever that may be."

Olivia's parents had an arranged marriage, like so many were. As high-strung and overburdening as her mother was, her father made up for it in his warmth and genuine love for his children. He cared not that he had only daughters, and encouraged them to do as they pleased. Olivia wished so desperately that she had the ability to follow in her father's footsteps. She enjoyed listening to him as he rambled on about running the estate, about the finances to be managed for the household, the debts and the repayments.

In turn, he had treated Olivia as he would a son, and she had been enthralled with his every word, as much as most young girls were with the latest fashions of the day. If only she was a man. Then she could not only take on his title and his holdings, but also live as she wished, doing what she wanted, when she pleased, without having to answer to anyone — to a mother or a husband, or to all that was expected of her by society.

"How did you begin on this latest scheme, anyway?" Rosalind asked.

"Scheme? You mean my writings for *The Register*?"

"Yes," replied Rosalind. "I hardly think it a natural circumstance for a young woman to be providing financial advice through a journal to the English gentry."

"I wouldn't say it's unnatural, but it is rather unusual," conceded Olivia. "My father subscribes to *The Financial Register*, you see, and I saw an article one day from a reader bemoaning his current situation. I wrote back to the journal with a response to him. I didn't sign it, but it was published, with a comment at the bottom asking for the mysterious stranger to get in touch with him. I did, but of course not as myself, but an assumed identity. And so P.J. Scott was born. The initials are from my grandmothers' names, and then Scott is simply in silent spite to my mother, who bemoans the bit of Scottish blood that runs through our veins from her own grandfather."

"Well, I for one am proud of you, Olivia," said Rosalind with a sigh. "It certainly must add some excitement to your life."

Olivia smiled. "It's wonderful, Rosalind — powerful even. You do remember, however, that you must tell no one of this. It is our secret and it must stay that way."

"Of course," Rosalind said. "You can trust me. Now, are you ready for Lady Sybille's coming-out ball next week?"

"I suppose," said Olivia with a shrug. "As much as I am regarding the rest of them,"

"Oh Olivia," said Rosalind. "You cannot think that way. You never know what's waiting for you if you pull your head out of your figures and take a good look around you!"

Lady Hester Montgomery chose that moment to join their conversation.

"Olivia, darling," she said with a smug grin. "Are you still trying to find yourself a husband? After how many seasons, do you suppose, is it time to move on and accept that your time has passed?"

"Oh do shut up, Hester," Olivia said with a roll of her eyes. "Why must you be such a witch at all times? You may not have as many seasons' experience as I do, however it is not as though you are a fresh daisy yourself on the marriage market."

Hester's lips rounded into an O as she looked down her nose at Olivia.

"That mouth of yours is becoming rather low-bred, Olivia," she said. "I should watch what comes out of it if I were you."

As she flounced away, Rosalind looked wide-eyed at Olivia, who was nonchalantly sipping her tea as if nothing untoward had occurred.

"You must be careful with Hester, Olivia," she said. "She's a right nasty one."

"Don't I know it." Olivia narrowed her eyes. "Never fear, Ros. I can handle a girl like Hester. I shall never understand why she feels she should be able to say such things to whomever she wishes. I do not stand for such women."

Olivia looked around her now. Mothers and daughters sipping tea and eating pastries, as they discussed one another's affairs, carefully guarding their words. Olivia always spoke her mind, which seemed to get her into more trouble than she bargained for. This was why she enjoyed her hidden identity. Under her guise with the journal, she could say whatever she wanted — as a man — and not have to worry about what she wrote.

If only life itself were the same.

\* \* \*

*Keep reading* He's a Duke, But I Love Him*!*

# ALSO BY ELLIE ST. CLAIR

*Happily Ever After*
The Duke She Wished For
Someday Her Duke Will Come
Once Upon a Duke's Dream
He's a Duke, But I Love Him
Loved by the Viscount
Because the Earl Loved Me

Happily Ever After Box Set Books 1-3
Happily Ever After Box Set Books 4-6

*Reckless Rogues*
The Earls's Secret
The Viscount's Code
Prequel, The Duke's Treasure, available in:
I Like Big Dukes and I Cannot Lie

*The Remingtons of the Regency*
The Mystery of the Debonair Duke
The Secret of the Dashing Detective
The Clue of the Brilliant Bastard
The Quest of the Reclusive Rogue

*The Unconventional Ladies*
Lady of Mystery
Lady of Fortune

Lady of Providence

Lady of Charade

The Unconventional Ladies Box Set

*To the Time of the Highlanders*

A Time to Wed

A Time to Love

A Time to Dream

*Thieves of Desire*

The Art of Stealing a Duke's Heart

A Jewel for the Taking

A Prize Worth Fighting For

Gambling for the Lost Lord's Love

Romance of a Robbery

Thieves of Desire Box Set

*The Bluestocking Scandals*

Designs on a Duke

Inventing the Viscount

Discovering the Baron

The Valet Experiment

Writing the Rake

Risking the Detective

A Noble Excavation

A Gentleman of Mystery

The Bluestocking Scandals Box Set: Books 1-4

The Bluestocking Scandals Box Set: Books 5-8

*Blooming Brides*
A Duke for Daisy
A Marquess for Marigold
An Earl for Iris
A Viscount for Violet

The Blooming Brides Box Set: Books 1-4

*The Victorian Highlanders*
Duncan's Christmas - (prequel)
Callum's Vow
Finlay's Duty
Adam's Call
Roderick's Purpose
Peggy's Love

The Victorian Highlanders Box Set Books 1-5

*Searching Hearts*
Duke of Christmas (prequel)
Quest of Honor
Clue of Affection
Hearts of Trust
Hope of Romance
Promise of Redemption

Searching Hearts Box Set (Books 1-5)

*Christmas*
Christmastide with His Countess
Her Christmas Wish

Merry Misrule

A Match Made at Christmas

A Match Made in Winter

*Standalones*

Always Your Love

The Stormswept Stowaway

A Touch of Temptation

For a full list of all of Ellie's books, please see www.elliestclair.com/books.

## ABOUT THE AUTHOR

Ellie has always loved reading, writing, and history. For many years she has written short stories, non-fiction, and has worked on her true love and passion -- romance novels.

In every era there is the chance for romance, and Ellie enjoys exploring many different time periods, cultures, and geographic locations. No matter when or where, love can always prevail. She has a particular soft spot for the bad boys of history, and loves a strong heroine in her stories.

Ellie and her husband love nothing more than spending time at home with their children and Husky cross. Ellie can typically be found at the lake in the summer, pushing the stroller all year round, and, of course, with her computer in her lap or a book in hand.

She also loves corresponding with readers, so be sure to contact her!

www.elliestclair.com
ellie@elliestclair.com

Printed in Dunstable, United Kingdom